Mary Williams was born in Leicestershire and attended Leicester College of Art where she trained as an illustrator. During a varied and colourful life she wrote and illustrated children's programmes for BBC Wales and worked as a newspaper columnist.

She began writing ghost stories as a young child, and has had many occult novels published. She has also written and illustrated children's books, and contributed a variety of short stories to anthologies.

She has been married three times and widowed twice, and now lives alone with her Burmese cats in Cornwall.

TIME AFTER TIME
AND OTHER STORIES

In this collection of mysterious short stories the recurring theme of 'time after time' is reflected upon with varying intensity, and in several as a haunting reminder of life's immortality. Time itself has little meaning in the wheel of eternity, and it is more than possible that the vital spark or soul of any human being could by chance contact that of another known to him or her in a previous existence on earth. Some stories concentrate on the effect of wandering apparitions about the ether and in all of them can be found love, tragedy, emotional yearnings and sheer terror.

Books by Mary Williams
Published by The House of Ulverscroft:

CHILL COMPANY
TARNEFELL
FLOWERING THORN
CARNECRANE
RETURN TO CARNECRANE

MARY WILLIAMS

TIME AFTER TIME AND OTHER STORIES

Complete and Unabridged

ULVERSCROFT
Leicester

First published in Great Britain in 1997 by
Robert Hale Limited
London

First Large Print Edition
published 1999
by arrangement with
Robert Hale Limited
London

'The Chair' first appeared in *Whisper in the
Night* published by William Kimber 1979:
© Mary Williams, 1979

British Library CIP Data

Williams, Mary
Time after time and other stories.
—Large print ed.—
Ulverscroft large print series: mystery
1. Ghost stories, English
2. Large type books
I. Title
823.9'14 [F]

ISBN 0–7089–4055–2

Published by
F. A. Thorpe (Publishing) Ltd.
Anstey, Leicestershire
Set by Words & Graphics Ltd.
Anstey, Leicestershire
Printed and bound in Great Britain by
T. J. International Ltd., Padstow, Cornwall

This book is printed on acid-free paper

For Amy

Contents

Contents

Time After Time

1

I first met William Ivory in London at a literary luncheon held at the Mirabelle in 1946, and the brief second of that glance between us was electric, filled with astonishment. It was as though life exploded in strange wild recognition. And we both felt the same. I knew it, although to my knowledge we had never seen each other before. He was well known, of course, as a critic, possessing a keen perception of character and talent — ironic when necessary — much sought after by many, though feared by those professing an ability they didn't have. Any hint of artistic pretence, he abhorred.

As well as literary fame he was a mountaineer of repute and, during his early youth — at the time of our first meeting he must have been in his forties — had climbed many of the great mountain peaks of the world. It was this fact, perhaps, that gave him a certain air of aloofness in company. I myself, already in my early thirties, had always felt the lure of hills and lonely places. It is a sensation hard to explain if you don't happen to possess it.

Physical? Or spiritual? Maybe a blending of both, and it could have been this that played a part in the sudden overwhelming surge of emotional affinity affecting our two selves. But not entirely. There was more. Much more.

The impact between us was broken by the passing shape of a rather large woman that gave me time to recover and move automatically into the chattering crowd of authors, agents, booksellers, minor celebrities and publishers, all gathered together to acclaim a new author's first novel. The venture had also attracted not only those immediately concerned, but anyone 'in the know' who'd been sufficiently lucky to get an invitation.

As a freelance columnist for the *Monthly Magnet* — a comparatively recently launched magazine — I'd been asked to attend. Books were very much my line. I'd even had a romantic novel of my own published the previous spring and, although it had neither made my name nor fortune, and my publishers were still out of pocket because of the advance, ambition sizzled on in me, with a determination to keep a healthy interest in the work of current authors.

I *had* to have my mind busy. My husband had been killed in a car accident two years before, when driving from the hospital where I'd had an operation.

I'd been shocked naturally. But we'd been experiencing a more than usual stormy patch in the past few weeks. You could say, I suppose, that the marriage had been something of a failure from the start — sexually, mentally and emotionally. And he drank. Why did we marry? Why does anyone marry? At the time it had seemed the right thing to do.

My mother had died when I was eight, and my aunt had taken her place in my father's home. He was a clergyman in a country village near Oxford. Life under my aunt's care had been sterile and constricting; but I'd loved my father, and when he succumbed one hard winter to an attack of influenza I was left restless and unhappy, finding there was no longer any emotional anchor to cling to. I was eighteen then. I'd had a few friends, of course — undergraduates and intellectual dilettantes with high-flown ideas of philosophy and the arts. But they offered no roots. Oliver Chase did. He was ten years my senior, good-looking, a solicitor with prospects, and I chose to fall in love with him. I say 'chose' because that is exactly what I did, although I did not, at the time, recognize the devious way my mind was working. He fell for me; I was attractive to look at, I suppose, in a certain way that one admirer had said was elusive, and had kept myself aloof from having 'an affair' or 'playing around'. Oliver probably thought it was time he settled down, and I appeared suitable. Perhaps I meant more to him than that; I don't know. But when I was twenty we married, and from the very beginning it was a terrible mistake. We weren't suited in any way at all. Eventually he found solace with another woman whom I found in the marital bed on my return unexpectedly from a jaunt to London. There was no illusion left.

We'd patched things up.

But —

There were so many 'buts'. Oh, we tried for a time, both of us. I don't blame him alone for the deterioration in our relationship. I suppose I too was at fault, if anyone can be blamed for finding out too late that they didn't love the one they'd married. The fact was that the end of any remaining bond between us was already in sight when I had to go to hospital, and the accident, though a sad end for Oliver, finalized things.

For a time I *had* felt somehow guilty in an obscure kind of way, and for this reason had spent the following few months writing my book. Its acceptance had surprised me, because I recognized its literary limitations. But its publication had put me in touch with *The Magnet*, giving me temporary employment while I decided what to do, and where to go. One issue was clear: I must leave Oxford.

It did not take me long to decide where to go.

The Welsh Marches.

I would find a cottage somehow near Abergavenny or Brecon, where I could be on my own, live close to nature, free to write what I wanted, and wander the misty valleys and lonely mountains when I wished.

The love and sense of place is a strange thing, elusive and potent; and all my life I'd been haunted by that strip of country where I'd gone for brief visits with my father. It was as though, at unexpected intervals, unknown forces and voices had whispered to me — 'one day you will go there again, return to the quiet valleys and distant peaks where your destiny lies'.

Destiny? The word may sound over-romantic, but I'd learned at a young age to keep inner resources of imagination to myself, finding a secret world in compensation for the loss of my parents. I was, perhaps, over-sensitive to places and people, and elemental forces and influences.

Even as I stood chatting at the Mirabelle on that far-off day, I was aware of change drawing very near. I was in the gathering, but not of it. The artifices and rivalries, the calculated pretences, the wit and smart humour of the intelligentsia already bored me profoundly. The strange, almost magical, though unspoken, communication with William Ivory therefore held a clarity and meaning — an acute awareness of my own identity. Competition and ambition were blurred into shadow. The colourful headgear of feathers and flowers and absurd wide brims became no more than a haze of misted shapes, and the wagging tongues a drone merely like the buzzing of bees in a far-off summer sky.

The floor beneath my feet seemed to tremble just for a second. Then I saw him approach, making his way purposefully past a well-known female crime writer. She had something on her bleached hair that looked like an immense hedgehog. She appeared briefly annoyed and turned with a swirl of a crimson cape-like thing over her shoulder to talk to a tubby, owlish, long-haired man with glasses. The chatter of voices and celebrating registered in my ears again. I pulled myself together and heard a voice saying clearly above the din, 'I think you're Leonara Darke?'

I stared for a moment, astonished, with a wild irrational joy surging through me. William Ivory's clear eyes were staring down into mine, his tilted lips curved up in a half-smile.

'Yes,' I managed to answer feebly, 'and you're — '

'William Ivory,' he interposed for me. 'I glanced through your book. Rather briefly, I'm afraid, and not quite my style. But it told me sufficient to realize that one day you'll do better. In other words, Miss Darke, don't be put off. Continue — creating, shall we say — ?' The suggestion of a smile died suddenly, and it was as though the intenseness of his impression was meant to convey something far deeper than any words possibly could.

'Thank you,' I replied. 'I'm quite flattered that you noticed any work of mine at all.'

'Don't be.' His manner was suddenly abrupt. 'I fancy we may have a good deal in common. Far removed from this sort of thing.' He gave a cursory glance at the hubbub of babbling figures and, during that split second, an aged lady in a floating dress, wearing lots of pearls and make-up, forced herself between us, with a volume of adulation on her over-red lips. 'Ah, Mr

Ivory,' she gushed, 'how *truly* delightful to see you — '

I moved away, and he was caught off-course. That was the last I saw of him then. But the impact on me of our encounter drove me in a frenzy of energy to speed up my plans for finding a cottage as soon as possible. There seemed no point in day-dreaming about William Ivory. I'd heard or read somewhere that he had a wife and family living in a country home that he visited at weekends. I didn't want any emotional entanglements or complications. One moment could be far more vital and enduring than reality. Our only possible future contact could be through books. That might happen; it might not. In the meantime, once I was settled I would write — something more than mere romanticism, but of enduring value. And then — well, who could tell?

So, that same week, I drove to Chepstow, put up at an hotel there for a period, and started my tour of the countryside.

After a fortnight's search I found it: a cottage that probably dated from Elizabethan times, having been built originally on an earlier site and renovated from time to time for farming purposes. It was situated in a valley of the Black Mountains, bordering

10

Abergavenny and Crickhowell near a cluster of buildings hardly large enough to call a hamlet but possessing one tiny shop. A small bus wound its way once daily for the delivery of post. Nearby were the ruins of what had been an ancient monastery in the far past, with an inn, The Castle Arms, constructed and rebuilt on one side. The clientele of the hostelry were obviously mountain farmers and occasional visitors wanting to explore and enjoy the solitude of the surrounding hills.

I knew at once that I wanted it.

This was the place.

Woodlands dotted the bases of the slopes which rose in humped misted shapes above the shadowed trees to distant peaks, converging from high dark ridges into the Brecon Beacons. The atmosphere held an air of secret history that was both an inspiration and challenge. A little stream tumbled its way past the narrow valley lane near the cottage. I visualized myself dabbling my toes in it and climbing the various steep tracks between furze and rocks, the sort of things I'd do at first, after I'd settled in — just live and absorb and enjoy.

Far, far away from the world of William Ivory.

After settling with the farmer who no

longer had use for the property, and who, strangely, asked a very low price, I returned to Oxford and told *The Magnet* of my decision to pack in the journalist rat race.

The staff, and the rest of my friends in the town, quite clearly thought I was mad.

'You'll go crazy on your own in such an out-of-the-way place,' a friend said. 'What will you do all day?'

She'd been with me at art school for a brief year before my marriage — a colourful, out-going character now based in London with a firm of commercial designers. She and her current boyfriend were talking of setting up a business of their own as dealers in modern stoneware.

'I might even paint a bit,' I'd told her, 'and write of course. Something creative. It will all depend.'

'On what?'

'What I feel like.'

She'd shrugged and turned away with a comment on her lips I didn't hear but I knew was uncomplimentary. Although we'd enjoyed, at certain times, a superficial comradeship, there'd never been closeness between us. Following my departure from Oxford and town life she'd remain in my mind merely as a bright picture of a racy, rather flamboyant, personality who could be amusing and slightly irritating at the same time, quickly fading into a limbo of passing memories leaving no ache, or emotional impact whatsoever.

And so it happened.

I left Oxford and London the following month, arriving on a fine evening in September at Brynteggan.

The sky was fading to a dying glow over the hills when I got out of my small car at the door of the cottage. Deep bowls of shadows filled the valleys, stretching towards Capel-y-Fyn on one side, in the other direction to Talgarth, Crickhowell and Brecon. Behind me was Llanthony. The high ridge on my right ahead must, I knew, overlook the Hereford plain.

Before inserting my key into the door I glanced back down the slope at the tiny hamlet almost hidden in a fold of the wild moorland. The dying light caught the glint of windows, and a thin spiral of smoke curled lazily from one chimney.

There was no wind.

The clustered woodlands skirting the valleys were hushed and still, holding a curious sense of watchfulness.

Like sentinels, I thought.

Guarding me; from what?

It was an eerie feeling, but not unpleasant.

13

Hadn't I always been haunted by that particular sense of place?

Well, now I was here; I'd found it.

I inserted my key and went in.

There was no hall, the entrance opened straight into the living-room, and the atmosphere was warm. There had been a fire burning in the old grate earlier, and a few embers still remained. Quiet shadows filled the interior with a sense of welcome, giving mystery to the alcove at the end of the room which led in a curving stairway to the floor above. On my right there was a door to the kitchen quarters and a small pantry-cum-outhouse. Most of the premises needed decorating, although the place had been kept reasonably up-to-date, and colour-washed in the not-too-far-off past. The one modern installation was a telephone.

'An artist lived here at one time,' Mrs Morgan, the farmer's wife, who'd owned it and first shown me round, had told me. 'But a strange sort of fellow he was, and didn't stay long. Funny really, no one ever does. It's the remoteness, you see — ' She added quickly, 'Cut off as it is. Of course, at one time it was just a barn. And before that — who's to say? One of those learned men, an archeo-archeologist, that what they call them? — *he* said the site was fought over hundreds of years ago, near a thousand maybe, taken by the plunderin' English. Then back again to the Welsh, an' then — but my dear life! you'll not be wanting to hear 'bout those cruel times. Here it is in Wales where it belongs. And you now. Is it any Welsh blood you have in you, my dear?'

Thinking it an odd manner of clinching a business deal, I'd nevertheless been able to answer, 'Yes, my grandmother was Welsh. She was born in Gwent.'

'Ah.' Her sigh of relief was audible. 'That's nice to know, that is.'

However unusual the process of buying had been, Morag Morgan had seen that everything about the cottage had been in spick-and-span order for my arrival.

It was already mostly furnished except for the larger of the two rooms upstairs, and some of my own bits and pieces from the flat were due for delivery the following day. I glanced round appreciatively at the genuine Welsh dresser standing in the background at right angles to the fire. Only a mug or two and plates were stacked there, but I'd brought my own few pots and pans along with other things, including a large rug that would be needed for the stone-flagged floor, linen and a colourful patchwork quilt for the bed. The deal table — at least I guessed it was deal — was covered by a brown velveteen cloth, and on it an earthenware jug of yellow and bronze chrysanthemums caught a last glimmer of fading sunlight. Beside it was a note written on a piece of paper. I picked it up and read:

There's milk in the kitchen and a loaf of bread. I've put a hot brick in the bed and you'll find logs and a bag of coal at the back. There's water laid on, as my husband showed you, with a tap. If it ever runs dry he'll bring you some from the pump. The stream's all right for drinking. Ebenezer — that's my son — will generally be around to give you a hand if you're in trouble. Mrs Jenkins at the shop will get in what you want for food if you go and see her. Remember if you want anything else tonight we're at the farm, Tygarth, just round the hill. Key of the back door hanging on hook of scullery shelf.
See you tomorrow.
Mrs Morag Morgan

A quaint note, but friendly and helpful, and although I appreciated the quietness and loneliness of the place, I was somehow grateful to know company was not far away if I needed it.

Before going out to the car for my bags and personal etceteras, I flung myself into a comfortably padded spindlebacked chair and relaxed for a brief few moments with a gratifying sense of fulfilment.

The shadows seemed to deepen and intensify around me; but despite the fitful glitter of occasional pieces of newly polished brass and glowing cinders, the atmosphere was of age and of times long gone. In that short space of time I almost slipped into a state of dreamy oblivion. Then the sudden cry of some wild thing outside roused me. I jumped up and went to the door. There was no movement, no stirring of any living thing through the quickly fading landscape. As I took my belongings from the car the last ray of dying gold slipped behind the mountain ridge opposite. Yet the air seemed full of soundless whispers from the trees below. I turned and lugged my cases through the doorway, filled with strange mounting excitement.

My new home.

And yet with its own identity that was more haunting and stronger than any human claim to possession.

So it was that I came to Brynteggan.

2

My first week at Brynteggan was spent mostly in adapting to the changed circumstances of living, of getting to know the few inhabitants of the area, and wandering the surrounding mountains. Those leisure hours were rich and heady, filled with a sense of enchantment and wonder. I had the frequent feeling of being in some mysterious hinterland bordering dream and reality that no words can adequately describe.

Never will I forget that first autumn in my new home. The mornings when pearly mist gradually lifted from the valleys, lit to transient gold from a rising pale sun, and evenings when the hills loomed in massed humped shapes against the greenish clarity of twilight.

It was easy then to imagine legends brought to life: of stories I'd read in the *Mabinogion* dealing with Killach and Olwen, Arthur, and the children of Llyr. Others too, unwritten about and unknown, but forever haunting that mysterious landscape ready to emerge in quiet unexpected moments. These perhaps I would recreate in a book, exorcising for good

18

what remained at the back of my mind of the compelling memory of William Ivory.

Yes, he was still there, however insistently I told myself he wasn't, and no doubt when my full story is told any who read it may accept the following events as a mere fabrication of an overwrought imagination. But I was not the only one to experience strange happenings at Brynteggan. There had been the artist; and, as the days passed, I became increasingly aware of growing half-furtive curiosity expressed by the few inhabitants I contacted, including the postmistress and shop-keeper at Llanbach not far away who, though friendly and pleasant from the first, could not conceal a certain query of surprise in her dark eyes when she asked on each occasion we met, 'And is it all right you are, my dear, at that little place by the hill?'

I gave almost the same answer each time. 'Oh, yes, thank you. I love it.'

'Hm! when winter comes you may feel differently. All who've been there before do. Lonely it is then with the dark nights and no electricity.'

'I like being alone,' I told her. 'That's what I came for.'

'Ah, but — ' She paused a moment, eyeing me closely before continuing, 'I didn't say you'd be alone now, did I, *cariad*?'

I was puzzled. 'What do you mean, Mrs Jenkins?'

But she didn't answer. Just shook her head and turned away to fetch the stamps I wanted. When she came back she evaded the subject, turning it to other more practical matters.

I didn't pursue the topic further. But as the evenings darkened, drawing in to earlier twilights, I did begin to understand what she'd meant by her allusion to my 'not being alone'. The atmosphere itself sometimes, though quiet, seemed almost a living entity.

By the middle of October, I'd formed the habit of going up to my bedroom in time to watch the evening light close over the hills. As everything became resolved gradually into a maze of blurred shapes and shadows, I'd light the oil lamp which stood on a round pedestal table near my bed, draw the curtains, and finally have a short read from one of the books I'd brought with me before undressing for sleep. But reading wasn't really easy in the muted light, and generally I had laid it aside by nine o'clock. Usually I slept well, partly due, I suppose, to healthy physical tiredness following the day's activities of walking, writing a little and digging. The cottage garden was proving quite a challenge, being at first a mere tract of ground covered by rough stones and furze. I contemplated transforming it eventually into a colourful rock garden at the front, and at the back for growing my own vegetables. However, I'd managed to clear a small strip one day when my spade struck something hard and more metallic-sounding than the usual granite. I'd done my best to prise it out, but feeling suddenly exhausted had left it for the time being, determining to have a go the next morning.

The following day rain fell during the morning, but in the afternoon the sky cleared, leaving the earth moist and tangy with the mingled smell of distant smoke, fallen leaves and all the nostalgic scents of the woodlands.

After a cup of tea, I went out, fetched the spade from the shed and got to work on retrieving — if possible — what might lie hidden in the damp ground.

I had to dig quite a hole and my effort was only productive because the soil had loosened from the rain. As the spade struck, a few stones rolled past my feet revealing the surface of something dark and glimmering secreted firmly, still, nearby.

After a further effort of heaving and prodding, with the perspiration dripping down my forehead, I managed to loosen the object and got it out.

It was round and quite heavy — blackened by the years, and the size of a saucer, but where the earth fell away glowing with glints of what could have been gold, or copper perhaps. Not being a student of mineralogy, I hadn't a clue which.

I brushed away the earth, and took it to the cottage tap to wash.

Curiosity and excitement swept through me.

A medallion.

Green mould dimmed much of the lettering which must have been inscribed in the far past, but two ancient letters, ES, and a number, 25, were decipherable.

My heart quickened. I knew instinctively a story lay in its identification — a story that in some mysterious way had become linked with my presence at Brynteggan.

Later, when I'd scrubbed and polished the relic, an ornate intricate pattern, including the legendary symbol of a dragon, was visible. I took it up to my bedroom that night, and stood with it in my hand staring reflectively out across the moon-washed landscape. The trees loomed hushed and motionless as watchful sentinels below the slope of garden and a strange feeling of expectancy, almost hypnotic, rooted my attention on their long shadows stretching towards the cottage.

The sensation was vibrant through my veins as though communication flowed between some unknown visitant and myself. Those brief strange seconds were broken only by the eerie crying of a bird through the dusk.

I pulled myself together sharply, and turned, letting the medallion fall to the floor. When I took one further look through the window there was no one watching there, nothing but shadowed shapes of the mountains beyond the trees and the deeper darkness of the valley. Quickly I drew the curtains, picked the relic up and placed it on the sill, telling myself I'd let my imagination run riot because of Mrs Jenkins' reference to my not being alone.

I didn't, as I'd previously planned, work in the garden the following day, but walked over the hills, bordering the tops of the mountains, to Capel-y-Fyn, where Father Ignatius, the eccentric and lone monk had once lived. There was a point not far away overlooking several counties, including Herefordshire, Monmouthshire and Gloucestershire. From where I stood reflectively for a few moments, Brecon lay to my left beyond Table Mountain. I was jerked suddenly round by the thudding of galloping hooves from

23

that direction. A number of wild ponies appeared on a ridge and involuntarily I swerved to one side, but they cut away abruptly to the east and soon disappeared in the early morning haze. Almost immediately a further horse cantered into view. But this time it had a rider. He brought his mount to a halt when he saw me and swung himself from the saddle.

'Hello,' he said. 'Good morning. You're early to be out up here — '

He was youngish, fair-haired and lively looking, wearing sophisticated riding kit that somehow seemed out of place in the surroundings.

'I live not far away and I like walking,' I told him.

'More than I do. But I guess I'm a bit of a lazy bloke.'

There was a pause between us. Something in me wanted to get away. He had a nerve, I thought, disturbing the dreamy atmosphere, breaking into my solitude when he'd never seen me before in his life. On the other hand, he was quite attractive, and the glance in his eyes was complimentary, without in any way being suggestive or over-intimate. As though sensing an inner curiosity in me, he remarked that he was in the district for business reasons; on location for a film.

My heart sank.

'Do you mean you're going to — to get crowds of people running about and littering the hills?'

He laughed. 'Steady on now. Not me — my crew. And there certainly won't be many. Just a very limited number, and no litter I can assure you.'

'Oh.'

'Well — I'll leave you now to get on with your wandering. Our headquarters for a week will be in Abergavenny. Ever go there?'

'Sometimes, if there's anything special I want for shopping.'

'See you perhaps one day. Have a drink with me or a snack at a place I know?'

'Oh. I don't think that's very likely.'

'Try and make it so,' he said with a grin. 'I'll be looking.'

He mounted his horse, gave a little gesture of farewell, and with a 'salut' was away.

At any other time I'd probably have been titillated by the suggestion of possibly getting involved with a film crew; but I was already so immersed with my newly found isolation that the idea made no impact whatever.

True, he was handsome, and no doubt much sought after by the female sex. His eyes, when the sunlight caught them had been very blue. Blue — a merry, healthy, ordinary blue. But the eyes I saw in memory when I allowed my thoughts to stray were quite different and of someone else, holding all the changing elusive shades of nature, from greenish brown to hazel, lit with translucent specks of gold.

Knowledgeable searching eyes. Desirous, too.

The eyes of William Ivory.

My spine shivered as his image, just for a second, seemed to sweep the landscape. I closed my eyes briefly; 'you must not' an inner voice insisted. 'Forget — forget — he is nothing to you, and never can be. Nothing — nothing — ' A little wind stirred, brushing the hair across my forehead. I turned, and walked back down the mountain, acknowledging, for the first time, that I was lonely.

That night there was a moon.

I was restless in my bed, and got up shortly after midnight, as I often did, for a glance through the window. The curtains were only half closed; I drew them wide, and the luminous light streaked pale over the silvered ground mist, giving a strange semblance of life to the grouped trees bordering the garden. A mounting excitement seized me, of what I knew not, until a hazy shape emerged and darkened through the dripping trunks. Rigidity claimed me; I dared hardly breathe, not through fear, but in anticipation of some powerful and elemental force quite beyond any logical explanation.

Unconsciously, my hand was resting on the medallion, and as my fingers tingled from increasing pressure, the shadowed shape took form and intensified. Just under the window it extended both arms as though embracing the night, and was still. My whole self became transfixed, held by the image which, though motionless and insubstantial, was real — so real to me I had no power to move or pull the curtains. I had no wish to, and no will. I simply stood there, watching. And then the head was lifted, and I felt the eyes on mine, compelling me. But I could distinguish no face. An intricate fretwork of branches hid everything but a glitter of light on a helmet or shining black hair. It could have been either.

Time died during the confrontation. I waited, half faint with tension. Then my hand shifted from the medallion to the wood sill for support. There was a quivering of the shape as a frail wind shuddered through the trees. A leaf fell from a branch of birch. Then all was still again. Nothing but the thin mist thickening over the moonlit pattern of the landscape and the rustle of some small wild thing below through the undergrowth.

I returned to bed, exhausted and shaking, knowing then the implication of Mrs Jenkins' prophetic words.

She glanced at me probingly when I called at the shop next day.

'Everything all right up there at Brynteggan, is it?' she asked, as she handed me a packet of biscuits.

'Yes, thank you,' I answered noncommittally.

'No visitors or unwanted callers then to trouble you?'

'I've seen no one,' I lied, not wishing to rouse gossip over the film crew.

'Ah!' she eyed me closely. 'But it's not only *seeing*, is it? There's listening you should be when the night falls on the mountains, and some things walk soft, *cariad*. Just take a care and remember we're here to help if you give a call.'

I took the bull by the horns and asked bluntly, 'Why are you trying to frighten me?'

'*Me?*' She gave a laugh. ' 'T'sn't me that would be frightening a body, oh dear me no. But there's things stronger than flesh and blood. Dark, secret things of the mountains and inheritors of the March. But you'll not be knowing of such like.' Her lips shut suddenly tight, and her eyes narrowed slightly, as though denying me contact.

'I know a good deal of the Welsh history,' I remarked a little tartly. 'My father was a scholarly man.'

'Not true Welsh though?'

'Half.'

'Hm.' She turned away abruptly. 'I must get back to the kitchen. Today's for baking. If you look in later before the light goes, I'll maybe have a cookie or two for you.'

'I'll try to come,' I told her. 'It all depends on whether I've time. I'm working in the garden now, and there's a lot to do.'

Nothing more was said between us on that occasion and, as things turned out when at last I put the spade aside that afternoon, I decided to leave the cookies for the following day. I was tired. More than just physically; it was as though all energy had been drained from me, leaving me so soaked in atmosphere that all I wanted was to dream away into forgetfulness the practical ordinary realities of living.

I went up to my bedroom earlier than usual and sat by the window making no attempt to read — merely watching the shadows deepening into twilight, as ideas for writing a book played idly, half-formed through my mind. The medallion lay glinting on the small table beside me; only half aware of what I was doing I stretched out my hand and touched it. Instantly a momentary shaft of light zig-zagged from the dusk outside and sent a second's wave of tingling life through my body. All my senses were alerted; I jumped up, focusing my gaze upon the tips of trees outside.

There was a curdling of the air and the shape was there, gradually looming larger, taking an ethereal substance through the foliage until it was directly beneath the window, concentrating attention upon my watchful figure which had become static from submission to a will more compelling than my own.

And still the face was hidden by a tracery of shadowed branches.

And yet I knew; knew the visitant was of tremendous import and identifiable as part of my deepest being.

How long the confrontation lasted I didn't know; when at last mobility returned, the scene, as before, had become bereft of any presence except the slipping shadows from pale moonlight between the fingered branches of trees, and humped bowls of distant hills.

★ ★ ★

30

During the following few days I left the relic carefully alone, and when evening came drew the bedroom curtains closed, not through fear, but because I felt in need of undisturbed sleep, after hours of walking mountain tracks and exploring the valleys of the foothills.

I took a trip in my car to Abergavenny one day, and was about to enter a bookshop when I saw the film men coming up the street. I dodged into a doorway, but the fair-haired man I had met on the hills spotted me.

'Hey?' he said, with his friendly grin. 'So you took my invite. Sensible girl.'

'Not exactly,' I replied, wincing, as he wrung my hand. 'I haven't much time.'

'Time for a quickie, I'm sure. Come along now. Don't be coy — Miss — or is it Mrs?' His voice died in a query.

'*Miss*. And my name's Darke. Leonara Darke.'

'Hm. Poetic. It suits you.'

Half hoping, as most authors do, even writers like me who'd had only one novel published, that he might have read it and recognized the name, I simply said lamely, 'Thank you.'

After those few words I rather weakly allowed him to usher me across the road into the bar of an hotel opposite — where we partook of pink gins and nibbled nuts and biscuits.

He was very friendly. I liked him; but when he suggested I might be an extra for the film project, I went suddenly very cold.

'*No*,' I said more vehemently than was necessary. '*No*. I'm sorry, I just couldn't.'

'What's the matter, for God's sake? Most girls would jump at the idea. And you've the looks and all it takes to impress the big boys. Good bone structure, fine eyes and a wayward elfin touch. Think again, darling.'

I didn't need to think. Wasn't that sort of approach to existence just what I'd done my best to escape from?

So I put my glass down with a sharp tinkle, stood up and said, 'Thank you for the aperitif, but I'm afraid I'll have to be going now. I've rather a lot to do, and — and I wouldn't really be any good in a film — not even as an extra.' There was a pause before I added, 'I'm sorry.'

For a moment the merry blue eyes went ice hard. 'No need to apologize, Miss Darke.' The handsome head gave a quick bow. '*Adieu* then. Or should one say *au revoir*? No, I fancy not. Never mind, nice to have met you.'

A minute later I was out in the street with the soft breeze on my face, feeling ridiculously that I had escaped from prison — the sophisticated prison of the past.

I bought notepaper, a new biro, and other odds and ends unobtainable at the local shop, then got into my car at its parking place and drove from the town up the main road leading to Brecon. I decided I'd have a meal *en route* at a certain historic hotel, famed for its comfort and good food, in Crickhowell, then take a look at the Beacons before making my way cross country from Brecon to Llanbach and Brynteggan.

It was six o'clock before I arrived at the cottage and from my first step inside the door I had a strange sensation of 'not being alone'. Mrs Jenkins' words flew to mind.

Eerie? Yes. But not unpleasant. There was even an intimation of welcome in the quiet shadows of early evening hugging the alcove of the fireplace and corners of the room by the dresser. Shadows that crept intriguingly and deepened in the stairway recess leading to the bedrooms.

There was no fire of course. But it was ready laid with paper, coal and logs, and I soon put a match to it and had a cosy blaze going. After that I made toast and boiled an egg — a fresh one from the farm — and had a light supper. When I'd finished and cleared away, I settled down comfortably poring over the magazines I'd bought in Abergavenny.

The light outside gradually faded from a golden sunset to an azure twilight. An owl called from nearby, followed by all the hushed mixed sounds of evening — a man's whistle from the lane below — probably a farm boy's, the trickle of the stream over the stones, the croaking of a frog, and the rustle of some small wild thing through the grass. The spitting of a log, sending a shower of tiny sparks followed by a tiny spiral of smoke into the air, emphasized there was no such thing as complete emptiness of atmosphere. With ears alerted I even fancied the soft tread of invisible footsteps outside. Or were they invisible?

I got up from my chair and went to the door, opened it and poked my head out. Nothing unexpected was to be seen; just the gentle dusk deepening over a film of ground mist and the moon's light above the horizon.

Yet as I stood there I became aware of some magnetic unknown force electrifying the atmosphere — calling me.

With a burst of willpower I shut the door and pulled the curtains close, and did not open them again that night.

The next day there was a wind that brought a thin shower of rain in the afternoon. But by the evening it had cleared, leaving the hills and mountains bright and shining.

I went to bed early and determinedly closed the curtains, pushed the small table to my bedside and lit the lamp. I had a book ready and when I'd washed, settled down between the sheets and started to read.

It was no use. The air was too warm and steamy after the earlier showers, and mingled with the dampness was a fragrance, an insidious perfume filling my lungs and senses with a strange nostalgic longing.

Against my determination to be normal and impervious to further imagination — for surely any previous weird experiences I'd had *had* been imagination — I got up and went to the window and, in pulling the curtains apart, inadvertently touched the medallion.

Then, as my eyes glanced out across the garden, I saw him.

He was there; a dark figure emerging through the trees gradually, but more definite this time, with his head turned upwards to my window. Instant communication flowed between us. My heart stopped for seconds, then bounded on again in wild irrational excitement and recognition. For that brief interval his face, though dimmed, penetrated through the shadowed trees, and it was a face I knew. A face that had haunted me unacknowledged for many, many days and nights.

That of William Ivory.

My senses froze. Froze with desire then flowered to meet him. But I did not move. Just stared, though his whole being called to me. I was still standing motionless when a wave of giddiness swept over me. The room seemed to swim round, and I only steadied myself by reaching for the windowsill. When I recovered he was gone.

I moved at last automatically, and glanced down. Instead of the medallion, words in a small pool of golden light glittered there. They were quivering, living words, and read:

When you are ready
I am there —
To weave the starlight
In your hair.
And crown thee with
Sweet eglantine
When you are mine — when you are
    mine.
Oh, come my darling — rich the night
That is reborn
For our delight —

I went for my notebook. The words were fading when I returned to the window, but I recalled what was there — indeed, the message had been engraved upon my memory for ever.

* * *

I did my best the following day to reason logically about the night's strange events, telling myself I must have been dreaming — that the verse, which had a medieval, or even more ancient touch about it, was a concoction of my own imagination resulting from over-tiredness in searching for the theme to found a book upon. Common sense in me insisted this must be so. There was no sign or mark of any inscription on the windowsill of my bedroom. The medallion lay in the exact position where I'd last seen it. The bushes and trees below showed no indication of having been disturbed. So what I *had* to do, I decided, was to accept the only practical explanation. In that case, had the sceptics about my leaving Oxford been right? Was living alone proving too much for me, and sending me off-balance, if not exactly mad?

The suggestion was unpleasant and mildly frightening. Obviously I needed some kind of company. Not necessarily the human variety but an animal of some kind — a cat or dog perhaps.

I remembered reading a notice in a shop window at Brecon which said, GOOD HOME WANTED FOR PET CAT. CLEAN, WITH AFFECTIONATE NATURE. Stimulated by the idea I set off in my car after an early snack lunch to have a look.

I discovered that the owner had died, and no one so far had made an offer.

'I think it's because he's not a kitten any more,' the shopkeeper said a trifle wistfully. 'Folk always go for the very young ones. But you can't say Caradawc's *old* — only three years, doctored, and well trained, too.'

'So that's his name — Cara — '

'Caradawc. Legend says there was a prince once of that name who could never be overcome. Look at him now. Isn't he handsome?'

Actually Caradawc looked a bit wistful. He was, I was told, half-tabby and half-Siamese, with a bushy tail, ginger ears and a ginger patch over one eye. His overall colour was a kind of reddish beige, with little tufts of hair sticking out, longer than the rest, at unexpected places. His eyes were brilliant green. Certainly a very individual-looking cat, wearing a sad expression that decided me at once.

I fell for Caradawc.

So it was that five minutes later we

were driving back in my car to Brynteggan, Caradawc in a cardboard box behind me, with a hole in it just large enough for him to poke his nose out and make occasional protests.

His voice also was unique.

I spent that night downstairs with him on the sofa, having arranged a toilet box for him in the scullery. After a first prowl round, and with the fire stoked up, he appeared to settle down, although I did not get a great deal of sleep.

The sitting-room faced the same way as the bedroom, and although at odd times I fancied shadows moved outside passing the curtained window, reason told me it could easily have been the pattern of leaves pressing the glass.

For the first week following Caradawc's arrival at Brynteggan, everything went smoothly. He adapted well to his new life, and turned out to have a good temper and placid nature — *mostly*. But he was sensitive, alert to any sudden and unusual sounds, and definitely affected by atmosphere.

During those first days with my new pet, I determinedly kept from fingering the medallion or making any midnight jaunt to my bedroom window. I decided to bury the relic again when I felt sufficiently energetic, telling myself this would be the end of the melodramatic incident — or rather, of the strange dream I'd experienced.

But things turned out rather differently.

An evening came — oppressive with the heavy yellow atmosphere of approaching thunder — when Caradawc was not only alert, but definitely uneasy, his bright green eyes narrowed under faintly flattened ears, bushy tail waving, whiskers stiff and bristling.

He refused his meal, and paced to and fro, backwards and forwards from sitting-room to kitchen, streaking occasionally upstairs. I did not encourage him to visit the bedroom, but he was intent on doing so, and while I was finishing off a few little domestic chores he disappeared and did not come down again quite as quickly as habitually.

I ran after him. He was standing at the window, back arched, and I could almost feel the electric wave of his anger as a low feline growl stirred the air.

I made a swoop and picked him up, careful to avoid even a quick glance at the window, although the curtain flickered faintly from my sudden spurt of movement.

I made the cat basket comfortable before the fire which still glowed, and put a saucer beside it filled with the creamy top from the milk jug.

'Now, Caradawc,' I said, as though he was human, 'settle down and be good. Give me a rest, do.'

His look was burning, holding all the cunning, calculating awareness of his kind. After a time, soothed by the warmth and milk, curled up with chin on paws, he slept.

I went upstairs to my bedroom.

A thin shaft of pale moonlight, almost white, streaked across the bedroom floor. Each movement of mine cast zig-zagged patterns of dancing light and darkness up the cream walls, playing tantalizingly from nooks and crannies to join the dark shapes of furniture and bedposts. The picture was that of some scenic ancient tapestry brought to life — or one resurrected from a play acted long ago. I waited briefly, uncertainly, just staring. Then with a force of will looked across the room to where my white nightdress was slung over a chair. Already a strange compulsion struggled in me to give way, and become swallowed up by the ancient magic history of 'place', to be not merely myself but a vital part of the haunting night.

I faced the challenge, saying aloud, not realizing that to be speaking at all I was admitting defeat — 'No, *no*. You are *you* — Leonara Darke. This is your cottage, and you're going to undress and go to bed like any normal human being in the twentieth century.'

I changed into night gear, and in turning caught a glimpse of my reflection in the white robe through the mirror. For a moment I was startled. Was that really me? That pale girl with the loose shining hair and the circlet on it? But there was no circlet; how *could* there be? It was just the moonlight. The moon was so very bright and the room somehow seemed darker than it had been, perhaps because there were so many stars outside. The sky was sprinkled — filled with them.

Impulse drove me to the window.

He was there: leading a horse by the bridle. He came pushing through the trees — resolute, intent; and I knew he came for me. And when he reached the window he raised his face to mine. For the first time it was *completely* unshadowed.

I went rigid; every nerve in my body froze. I could neither look away nor move. His cap of black hair was a shining helmet. But the rest held only horror. The lines of his countenance were the gaunt bones of a skull with holed eyes pierced with tiny sparks, teeth shining in the clenched jaws. A scream came from my throat, echoed by the wild feline shriek of Caradawc as he streaked up the stairs to join me. I closed my eyes momentarily.

When I opened them again a puff of cloud dimmed the white moonlight and, as it cleared, the haggard skeleton visage went with it, like a mask blown away. The empty eyes grew warm and brilliant, flesh transformed and covered the shining bones, and the face below me, smiling and beckoning, was a face I knew.

The face of William Ivory.

★ ★ ★

What followed was like a dream in which one moves — gliding rather than walking — impelled by a force beyond and more powerful than human will to resist. I was aware, vaguely, of Caradawc's wailing as I drifted downstairs and out of the front door. The air was heavy but sweet with the mingled perfume of evening and fallen leaves. My senses flowered to meet him. The soft breeze brushed my face, and my breasts rose with urgency above the gold kirtle of my gown, for his embrace. And so I stood, with the diaphanous cloud of muslin silvered by night dew, entranced and waiting.

He came then, proud and magnificent in his manhood, wearing boots and a jerkin, with a dagger bright and shining in its sheath slung from one hip, and I knew that for this moment I had been born. I lifted my face and his lips were on mine; sweet, so sweet — the ecstasy was pain, like the pain of dying.

'My love,' he murmured. 'My love — my love.'

Nothing mattered any more but him. Nothing. There was a faintness and darkness, as my life's blood burst in a fountain of delirious delight in which the heart temporarily stopped beating. A second later he was speaking in a strange language that I nevertheless understood.

'I have to go now,' he said. 'This is the last time we shall meet in this world. But I am Llewellyn's man, *cariad*. I have to go. We shall meet again though — as we have met before — another sphere — another time — ' His voice was growing fainter. 'It is Nemesis — farewell — ' the air was suddenly chill. Before my eyes his features were disintegrating. I didn't look, but put a hand over my forehead, and when I let it drop there was no one there any more — only the dark night and the stars fading quickly, one by one, until all was black.

Then I fell.

★ ★ ★

When I recovered consciousness I was lying on the floor of my bedroom beneath the window. Something cool was brushing my forehead. I heard a gentle 'mew', and opening my eyes saw two green eyes staring at me from a furry face. Caradawc's. His paw was raised to touch me again. I managed to lift my head slightly and the tip of his tongue touched my cheek.

I felt I had risen from the dead. My heart quickened. I sat up and realized I was cold, shivering. For a few moments I was confused. Where had I been? How had I got back to the bedroom? What had happened? Then slowly I remembered the visitation and events of the night. The rider with the skull's terrifying face who'd turned into something else and claimed me with his kiss from some other darker world beyond time and space and understanding.

A stranger, yet one whom I'd known forever and always would, bound by a destiny more compelling than any earthly bond — to meet and part, and meet again, time after time, until we reached the portals of eternity.

Was this true? During the hours that followed the question haunted me. Could our lives — mine and William Ivory's — have been so intricately interwoven? Part of some vast cosmic pattern stretching beyond the limitation of physical life and death?

My mind reeled.

When dawn came I pulled on a wrap and went downstairs, to make a cup of coffee and toast, still questioning. It would have been so much the easiest course to gull myself that I'd been suffering a series of nightmares. I knew this would be the logical explanation given by friends and any who heard my story. In the first place, how could my phantasmagoric visitant have been William Ivory? He lived elsewhere, near London, with his family. He was a sought-after brilliant writer and critic, very much of this world, so the dark knight of my weird experience *must* have been imagery only. This is what any sane, sensible person would say.

But no. *No.*

As I thought back again, just for a second or two, the rapture, the sweet agony of our past contact swept through me and I almost caught the drift of night perfume on the air, felt the pressure of his lips in the brush of the freshening wind.

Then, just as quickly, the sensation passed, leaving me cool, and for the first time since I arrived at Brynteggan, strangely detached.

Whatever had happened I was still alive, and able to think and reason. Fortified and calmed by the knowledge, I had something to eat then and said to Caradawc, 'You can stay in your basket, or go for a prowl, Caradawc. I'm going for a walk on my own down to the shop to fetch the weekly paper. Shan't be long.' Exercise and fresh air might properly revive me, I thought.

So I set off for Llanbach.

Caradawc, being a cat, had his own ideas on the subject and followed me in fits and starts, tail waving, hoping possibly there was something in it for him — a tit-bit.

'Is that creature yours then?' Mrs Jenkins enquired, looking suspiciously at Caradawc, who was soon nosing round the small interior when I arrived.

'Yes. I got him in Brecon,' I told her. 'His owner had died.'

'Hm! — well, take a care he doesn't get shot then.'

'Shot? *Why*? Why should he be?'

'They're having trouble at the farm; Tygarth. Foxes getting the chickens and eggs, and that cat's got the look of one, with his colour and tail.'

'I keep him in at night. But thank you for warning me.'

She shrugged. 'It's a dog you should have

been having,' she said, 'something to protect you all alone up there. Still, there's no accounting for taste.' She dived into what appeared to be a confusion of papers and chose the right one as if by magic. Mrs Jenkins was an adept at producing order from chaos. I'd seen her more than once thrust a hand into what appeared to be a complete muddle of envelopes and forms and the next moment have what was asked for.

Minutes later I was on the walk back to Brynteggan.

Before I opened the door I heard the phone ringing. There was no sun that afternoon and the sound of the insistent 'bleep-bleep' from the empty cottage gave me a brief eerie feeling.

I hurried in and grabbed the receiver.

'Hello — '

'Hello,' a voice said in reply, a woman's voice.

'That you, Lee?'

I sagged with relief. Who I'd expected I didn't know. It was my friend from London.

'Glad you're still alive and ticking,' the voice said. 'I was rather wondering if you'd fallen off a mountain top or gone mad and drowned yourself. How are you, anyway?'

'Oh, I'm OK — and you?'

'Up to date so far, although some of us

48

aren't — one in particular.'

'What do you mean?'

'Ivory. William *Ivory*.'

My heart jerked. 'What about him?'

'So you haven't heard? Well, I don't suppose you would. Too soon to be in the local rags. He's dead.'

I was suddenly struck cold and numb. I couldn't speak until she continued, 'Hey! Are you there? Can you hear?'

I pulled myself together, and felt my heart bumping on again. 'Yes. *Yes.* But what did you say — William — William *Ivory* dead? But — '

'It's true. He was thrown from his horse yesterday evening apparently.'

'Where *was* he?' I interrupted.

'Where? Oh, I don't know exactly. Having a canter — somewhere near his home. He always goes for weekends, doesn't he? To be with his family. Anyway, there was this accident. Something frightened the horse and he was thrown. It was instantaneous — he hit his head and that was it. A shock for the literary world. And his poor wife. They were devoted from all accounts.'

'Oh dear,' I managed to mutter.

'What did you say? Your voice isn't clear.'

'I said 'oh dear'.' Wanting to scream I added more loudly, 'What *is* there to say except I'm sorry — all the usual things. After all, we weren't family friends or anything. Look, I'm a bit tired and this line's poor. Suppose we have a chat later?'

'Oh, if it's like that. Sorry to have disturbed your solitude.'

'Don't be shirty. I've a migraine actually.'

'Why didn't you say before? All right I'll go. Just thought I'd let you know the news. 'Bye.'

There was an abrupt click and contact was broken. I put the receiver down and flopped into the armchair. My hand was shaking.

At first I was too dazed to think at all coherently. How could it be? With last night and all the other nights preceding it, when William Ivory — or the *image* of William Ivory — had materialized at Brynteggan?

Llewellyn's man.

I recalled again with a shudder, the very last time — this momentary picture of the ghastly skull's face beneath the black hair, the fleshless bones and gaping jaws before the softened features dispelled horror by assuming the character of Ivory. Our mutual recognition and passionate interlude before he said 'farewell' to me and the world.

Had it *really happened*? That by some out-of-the-world unknown psychic force I'd been granted contact with someone who'd existed centuries ago — yet one who'd lived and breathed again in the present? Had our meeting at the Mirabelle been a macabre kind of collision between two souls who'd met and loved before? A sort of chance in millions?

There could be no proof.

If I related my story it would be ridiculed. The William Ivory I'd met was now gone, although when I closed my eyes the memory of his compelling kiss, and the flame of his eyes, rekindled the fire in my blood and heart.

Just for a brief interim, sitting in the quiet cottage, a wave of aching despair and loss overwhelmed me. Then, very gradually, it lifted into numbed acceptance.

I roused myself and opened the newspaper. It was there — in the 'Stop Press' column, two lines — 'William Ivory, the famous literary critic, killed in tragic accident'. I put the paper down. There'd be full reports to follow, of course, and no doubt something about him on the BBC. But no one would know the full story. No one could, because I would never tell it.

For a time I sat watching the clouds through the window drifting hazily across the grey sky, letting idle thoughts cross my mind, recalling Mrs Jenkins' words which had seemed so full of foreboding. But perhaps, after all, there'd been a sort of wisdom in her warnings. Life in this world was for the living, not ghosts, and maybe I should use the cottage just for short periods instead of full time. I was still young enough to have a full and creative existence ahead, apart from moors and mountains.

It was an idea, anyway.

Presently I got up and went to the bedroom.

The medallion still lay on the windowsill, but it was dulled and ordinary-looking and had no glow. I picked it up; it was very cold and made no contact.

Caradawc came bounding up the stairs.

'It's all right,' I told him, 'we're going to bury this now, boy. Come along, Caradawc.'

The cat rubbed his face against my leg, then gave a little leap, and together we went into the garden.

The hole I made was dark and deep and on top of the relic I pushed a piece of granite, sufficient to keep it safely entombed from the forces of wind and rain, and the ache of memory.

Forever, in this life.

Though, at times, I knew a fleeting echo might return as a frail whisper of what-might-have-been.

Fear

It was at Chrissie Beck's housewarming party that a mischievous remark of Charlie Blunn's started the following unfortunate train of events, though no one could blame him factually for what occurred. But Charlie happened to be what, in a past age, would have been dubbed as a smart Alec, with a liking to impress women, and a habit of getting a laugh at someone else's expense; in Chrissie he sensed a gullible victim.

Chrissie was a new employee at the firm where he worked, a comparatively unsophisticated character who'd moved to a flat in the town from the country to be nearer her work. The flat was on the first floor of a converted house in a suburban row, No. 3.

The guests assembled there on that fateful evening consisted of five fellow employees, including Charlie, and two friends from her schooldays.

Chrissie herself was nineteen years old, sensitive, ambitious, and fundamentally shy — the last a weakness she did her best to hide under a pretence of being blasé, modern and very much 'with it'. For the evening in question she'd had a special hair-do styled in pink and green spikes — it was the period for coloured locks — and wore a beaded black velvet top that reached to just a foot below the navel, over green tights. This was partly to impress — partly to defy the tradition of her old-fashioned country upbringing, under the somewhat severe discipline of a widowed aunt. Also, hopefully, she might attract a boy-friend; she had already perceived Charlie's ruminative glance upon her during her first fortnight with the firm, Willoughby Bros.

The event was on a Saturday, and she'd spent the morning and afternoon preparing and dressing for it. Her whole being was seething almost to fever pitch before the little crowd started to arrive. The apple-green wooden Alice-in-Wonderland-looking chairs made by a local carpenter were in place; coloured cushions covered the shabby spot on the sofa which she'd bought at a sale, and plates of sandwiches, some even containing caviare, were arranged invitingly on one end of the table. At the other end were bottles of white wine and one of sherry, Bristol Cream — everything expensive and more than she could really afford, but she'd been a 'bit of a devil', and spent her meagre savings on what was surely a good cause.

A last passing glance at her reflection through the looking-glass before the guests arrived was at first almost frightening — she very easily got frightened — then slowly reassuring. She was completely unaware of the dazed, rather lost-little-girl look staring out from her huge eyes.

But when Charlie Blunn arrived he sensed this immediately.

'Say!' he said, a few minutes later, 'you look great. A real pin-up. What we've been wanting around here for a long time.'

He was nothing much to look at himself, but his exotic T-shirt, scarlet jeans, breezy confident manner and air of owning the world, offset his pallid poor skin, weak chin and slightly protruberant eyes.

Chrissie felt a tell-tale blush stain her cheeks. She didn't know whether to be conventionally annoyed, or gratified. The latter won.

'Thanks,' she said.

After that it was easy.

For the first part of the evening, of course, she was busy handing round plates, serving coffee, and seeing no one was short of sandwiches or the tempting savoury biscuits and rolls. Charlie undertook responsibility for the alcohol, seeing no one's glass was empty until the bottles were at low ebb. The latest disco cassettes had been brought along with a recorder by a very junior executive of the firm and, as the hours passed and the general mood gradually relaxed into a deliciously dreamy sense of half-oblivion, Charlie made a point of wheedling his hostess into a comparatively intimate corner of the lounge where it was possible to display his usual talent.

'You know what I think of you,' he murmured, with his damp breath against her ear. She shivered a bit, but made no objection. After all, she had to behave like a sophisticated adult. 'I told you, you're great,' he continued huskily, 'but more than that — brave. That's what you are. A brave girl. Coming to live *here* — after what happened —'

She pulled away and stared at him. The mascara was running slightly from one eye where he'd briefly kissed it, and her heart was thumping wildly. She looked more than ever like a child dressed up.

'What do you mean? *Here?*'

His damp lips made a round 'O'.

'This place, darling. Not many girls would have the guts.'

'Why?'

Then he delivered his shock.

'The ghost. Mean you don't know?'

'*Ghost*?'

'Of the murderer, love. It was a long time ago, before the war, but he killed women, strangled them, and shut them in a cupboard. He was caught and — ' There was a nasty pause in which Charlie drew his right forefinger across his throat, and made a hissing sound. 'He was *executed*, love, and didn't like it one bit. Ever since, they say he comes back at times looking for more.'

Chrissie felt slow terror rising in her, although she knew she should ignore him.

'I don't believe it,' she said, easing away. 'You're wrong. There's no such thing as ghosts, and they'd have told me, the — the house agents. They wouldn't have let the flat if — if there was anything wrong, and anyway, how *could* he come back? Even if the murders *were* here — ?'

Charlie shook his head sombrely.

'Ah, that's the question isn't it? Wings? To be or not to be? You never know the means spooks have of returning.'

Chrissie jumped up. 'I don't want to hear any more. I'm — I'm going to forget it just as though you'd never said anything.'

' 'Course you are, love, you're *brave* as I said. I shouldn't fancy you if you were the scared sort.' The truth was, of course, she

59

was already how he wanted her.

The girl Chrissie was currently sharing an office with left the sofa and came towards her.

'What's the matter?' she asked. 'Is Charlie up to his tricks again? Don't listen to him. He's drunk anyway.'

'He said . . . he said — ' But the words just wouldn't come. 'Anyway — ' Chrissie swallowed nervously. To repeat such a story would do no good. If it was true about the murderer, what was the use? And if it wasn't she'd only look silly. So she muttered thickly, 'Oh, nothing. It's . . . I suppose I shouldn't have had that last sherry.'

Shortly after this the visitors began to leave.

But the effect of Charlie Blunn's revelation remained.

Chrissie did not sleep that night, but after the clearing up next day and partly through reaction, exhaustion sent her into a heavy slumber on the next night, and when she woke she made a firm resolve to pin down Charlie Blunn about the murders when she got a chance to see him alone. He *could* be kidding, although it wasn't a nice thing to do. Anyway, there were no such things as ghosts, she told herself determinedly, and if there *had* been such a horrible business in the past it must have been a very long time ago, or she'd have heard of it. So what was she frightened of?

It was just that everything had seemed so nice before, she thought reasoningly, a new job, a new boy-friend — possibly — and a place of her very own to call home. Well, she was not nearly so sure about the boy-friend now. A really *nice* friend would have kept a thing like a murder to himself. Perhaps the pink and green hair had done it, though. It could have made him think she was that type of girl — sensational.

She sighed. Oh, well, you lived and learned. Luckily the good wash she'd given her short-cut hair had brought most of the stain out. What a mercy she'd not used a permanent. Her natural light brown shade obviously suited her better.

She got to the office that Monday morning a little earlier than usual to catch Charlie on his own, but found he was not coming to work for a fortnight; he'd gone to Brighton for a holiday.

She felt frustrated, not merely through not seeing him but by being unable to get *facts* from him. A sneaking suspicion was forming in her mind that whatever had happened at No. 3 in the past, he'd certainly exaggerated. Must have. She thought of asking her new girl-friend about it, the one who'd warned her about Charlie at her party. But her natural shyness stopped her. Marianne — her name was currently fashionable at that time — might think her stupid for giving his story serious thought. There was the estate agent, of course. She could call there. But then the estate agent might snub her in a cold, impersonal, business-like way, and say it wasn't her affair *or* his what happened in a house more than fifty years ago.

She so desperately wanted to be properly mature and sufficiently worldly to cope with any stupid tale told by a thoughtless office clerk.

And that was what she tried to believe it was — a stupid tale.

During the first few days of Charlie's absence she retained a stoical silence concerning the murders and reported ghost. But locked away in her inmost mind, fear lingered, and at varied times during the evenings seemed to assume a presence of its own looming in the shadows of corners — especially in the bedroom where the wardrobe stood at right angles to the bed. Certain of the larger furniture had been available for the monthly sum paid in rent. She hadn't wanted it because it was heavy, old-fashioned, but she'd had no choice, and she'd done her best to brighten it up with her own pieces, and bought rugs, curtains and cushions.

On impulse, one late afternoon, her resolve of silence broke down. At the end of the road leading to No. 3, near the bus stop, was a small sweet shop where she occasionally bought chocolate. The owner was a talkative, elderly little woman who was generally ready for a brief gossip, and when Chrissie called on that certain occasion, and as casually as possible mentioned that she now occupied No. 3, Primrose Row, interest was immediately forthcoming.

'So you're the new tenant,' the little lady said. 'Fancy that. I've seen many changes there. My granny lived quite close when I was a little one. Of course, they were proper houses then. Not flats as they call them. Mostly private people although one or two took in lodgers. I hope you'll like it there.'

This gave Chrissie her opportunity.

'Someone said there was a murder there in my flat once,' she remarked, as lightly as though she was referring to a 'grocers' or 'chip shop'.'

The little woman screwed her eyes up thoughtfully. 'At No. 3? Why yes. I seem to recall someone saying so at one time.

But it must have been way back before the war, sixty or seventy years. Whether it was there or at the house next to it I don't really know.' She paused before adding, 'No use dwelling on such nasty things, is it, my dear? Happiness is for young people like you. Look forward to the good and forget the bad.'

But this was something Chrissie could not do. And that night the haunting began.

It was October, and yellowing skies deepened early to evening, hugging the rows of rooftops and chimney pots to a leaden misty uniformity that held a suggestion of approaching fog. Except for the thrum of distant traffic, everything seemed very still — ominously so to Chrissie's strained nerves. Some sign or sound of other occupants of the adjoining premises would have helped. But they were mostly used for business purposes, and the tenant of No. 4 worked on night duty in a hospital. There was an ache of loneliness emphasized by fear at the pit of her stomach as she inserted her key into the door. The few steps leading to the short hallway appeared in menacing darkness, causing her spine to stiffen when she couldn't at first find the light switch. At any moment it seemed to her the shadows would shuffle into movement towards her. She made an effort and stretched an arm further up the wall. There was a click and a blaze of light. Her heart started up again, bounding quite painfully against her ribs. When she reached her lounge she slumped on to the sofa and felt the cold sweat trickling down her face and neck. It took her some minutes to recover, and then she chided herself for being a coward and idiot.

'You're just tired,' she told herself scornfully. 'It's the party, and the new job, getting used to things, and all Charlie's fault for telling you about the murder. Be sensible now. Be more like Marianne — ' At this point she broke off and laughed, because she found she was talking aloud. But it was not happy laughter.

That evening she kept all available lights on until, following a quick supper, time came to go to bed. She then made certain the key was properly turned in the front door, undressed, had a wash, and switched the lights off, after seeing the water wasn't dripping, and the gas tap turned off safely — there seemed so many *small* details to attend to, just to be perfectly *sure*.

But sure against what? she thought, chiding herself. Murderers? Ghosts? But the locks of all the flats were safe against any intrusion, and ghosts didn't exist anyway. Did they?

Involuntarily she shivered as she went into

her bedroom clutching the book she was carrying tightly under her arm. Now why did she even have to wonder about such stupid things as hauntings and the madman Charlie had said came back from the dead sometimes to strangle more women, and put them in a wardrobe?

Wardrobe!

She glanced at the cumbrous piece of furniture when she lay in bed minutes later with her bedside lamp burning and knees up, the book propped open against the quilt. It was such an ugly thing; and *old* — it could have been even Victorian. Had it been there, she wondered, ever since the house was built? Had the *murderer* used it? The very idea terrified her.

The atmosphere slowly seemed to grow icy cold. She tried to relax and concentrate on the story before her that was an adventurous love tale; but it was no use. She switched off the light and closed her eyes tightly, trying to press complete darkness against her lids — darkness free from menacing shadows of lusting evil. That didn't work either. She pushed the switch on again, eyes and ears watchful, on the alert, nerves strained. Little creaks and sighs filled the room. She sat up abruptly, imagining she heard the soft pad of footsteps on the landing. It was as though her whole body had become petrified into immobility.

And then she saw it.

Nothing concrete — no form — just the slow movement of the door knob turning, and a whispering sighing sound in the air. To and fro, to and fro, for quite a minute it continued, until all was still once more, leaving nothing but an echo of sly insidious laughter, and *fear* — fear so smothering she could hardly breathe.

Was that how those poor women felt before the strangler killed them, she wondered, when thoughts could once more register in her mind? She lifted a cold hand to her neck and shuddered. It was no use telling herself that she'd turned the key in her bedroom door, that no one could get in without a noise, that she'd have time to reach and open the window and scream for help — ghosts weren't human, ghosts had ways of *returning*, they could get through doors and walls. She remembered what Charlie had said — but no, she didn't, quite — *what* was it he'd said? — but she mustn't think of it, she mustn't *try* to remember.

It was about two o'clock when she summoned sufficient courage to go to her small kitchen and make a cup of tea.

After that she spent the remaining hours

until morning on the couch in her lounge and managed to have a period of exhausted sleep.

In the morning, before going to the office, she did her best to appear normal, held cold wet pads to her eyes to disguise the tiredness, and applied more make-up than usual. She put on an air of brightness for her colleagues, and if any of them noticed a certain tension they said nothing.

When she returned to her flat in the late afternoon a dreary twilight was settling in, predictive of rain later. She opened the front door with a sinking doom-like feeling and her heart lurched as a figure emerged from the main corridor. But it was only the hospital worker setting out for her night shift a little later than usual.

Chrissie gave a little gasp of relief. 'Oh! It's you,' she said rather shrilly.

The woman laughed. 'Who did you think it was? Thieves?'

'No. Of course not — I just wondered — '

But the woman didn't want to hear what she wondered, merely pushed by, saying, 'Ta ta. Can't wait. 'Bye.' And she was gone.

Chrissie put her key in the door.

So she was quite alone again.

Alone except for the sounds she herself made — the metallic trickle of water as she ran it into the kettle, the echo of her own voice in her ears as she forced herself to hum an old tune, and the tread of her footsteps on the kitchen floor. Ordinary everyday sounds that you wouldn't notice generally, but, of course, she was terribly overtired. So tired, the light when she switched it on, dazzled in little spots before her eyes.

She held a dark piece of material over her eyes, and lay back on the sofa. This helped a little, but the sense of strain, of terrible anticipation remained. She was too tired to cook a meal that evening, not even to scramble an egg or make cheese on toast, but had a hot drink with biscuits, then went to bed, hoping desperately for a good night's sleep.

It was not to be.

At about ten o'clock, just as she was managing to relax a little, the threatened storm broke with a spatter of raindrops against the window and rumble of distant thunder. She sat up, startled, feeling the familiar pumping of her heart against her ribs. Blindly she reached for the light switch. Then she remembered it was safer not to use electricity in a thunderstorm, and put it off again.

There was no wind, and the calm background to the increasing tap-tap of rain made the atmosphere somehow more ominous. Following the first flash of lightning she put her head under the duvet, consumed by fear and a sense that something terrible was about to happen. But there seemed no air to breathe. Her lungs felt choked, and her throat was dry. She put a hand to the pit of her neck and pushed her head out.

Then she saw it.

Outlined against the window, lit momentarily by a further flash of light was a broad form moving steadily but purposefully towards the towering shape of the wardrobe near the foot of her bed. The door of the cumbrous article swung open revealing masks of faces, dead pale faces, swinging against the shadowed interior.

Chrissie tried to scream, but no sound came. The figure turned, its evil lusting stare upon her, thick lips wide and smiling, one hand stretched and grasping, fingers writhing snake-like through the cloying air.

There was a moment of terrified awareness before 'the thing' reached her neck. Then fear itself obliterated everything that was living in Chrissie Beck and unconsciousness finally and mercifully claimed her.

She was dead.

At the inquest, it was stated that she had died of a massive heart attack. A peculiar feature of the case was that there were thin red marks similar to strangulation around her neck, but they were proved to be entirely superficial. There was no evidence whatever of any physical contact or attack.

To her colleagues she was known to be of a nervous and shy character, and the medical report said she was not strong and could have been affected by the stress of her new job and the thunderstorm.

The owner of the nearby sweet shop confided to a customer that the poor young thing had only recently brought up the long-ago tragedy of the wardrobe murderer, 'but I'd made a mistake saying it could have happened at *her* flat,' she said. 'I was trying to recall what my old granny had said, but *that* wasn't at *Primrose Row* at all, it was at the *next* street, *Daffodil Row*. Still it makes no difference.'

Charlie Blunn shrugged when he heard.

'Poor little drip,' he remarked casually, 'but she hadn't much spunk. Let's hope the next one's more promising.'

[I]gnore of the case was that there were able
to triple similar to imagination actions he
needs, and they were proud to be killed
heavier. There was no evidence whatever
of any ... ritual dealing or other.

... the blind happened, it was known to be
an essentially change e and the position
report and she was not strong and could have
been selected for the suitable person who ...
the thunderstorm.

The owner of the ... weakly ... store
confided to a customer that the poor young
thing had only recently brought on the lo-
... history of the windtobe murdered. 'Bot
I'll make a miserable anyone ... could have
happened to her dog', she said. 'I was trying
to recall that my old granny had said 'not
that night in a Tennessee town all it was at
the race shop 'no now how', said, in my ...
so attractive.

Charlie Ritch shrugged when he heard.
'Everything', he remarked casually. 'I'm
glad she had a much spirit. I do hope the
next one's a nice caring killer.'

The Echoing Dusk

Wildgrove stands deserted and empty now in its hollow; briars and weeds entangle its gaping windows and ivy clambers the crumbling walls.

Once it was different.

When the young Claverings took possession following their honeymoon, there were parties and laughter. The atmosphere was rich with love. But that was long ago. More than fifty years.

Before the war.

Happiness lasted for six months.

In the early days of the war, young Captain Guy Clavering was killed by enemy action, and ironically Lucinda, his wife, met her death from a heart attack on the same day when a bomb blasted the west wing of Wildgrove.

For a long time the ancient mansion was unlived in, left to nature and the elements. Whispers got about in the nearby village that it was haunted. Tales were spread of shadowy figures being glimpsed in the surrounding woodland at the far end of the grounds, and of distant singing and muffled laughter when the winds were in a certain direction.

But wild flowers blossomed in the erstwhile gardens. Occasionally children went there to pick bluebells, although discouraged by their elders with superstitious stories.

Nothing actually frightening or evil about the area had been suggested. It was just — somehow not like the rest of the countryside. And local people resented anything abnormal. The vegetation was more lush than the surrounding fields and lanes beyond the broken-down gates, the flowering cherry trees and wild apple blossom more profuse.

Why?

The question remained unanswered, and every year that passed a few more bricks fell from a chimney or a wall — until the day Elinor and Rupert Franklyn discovered the property on a holiday to the district.

At the first glimpse of the building crouched grey in the dip beneath the wood of larch, oak and spreading copper beech, Elinor, in particular, was entranced.

'This is it,' she said, after a few gasps of wonder and approval. 'We must have it. It's just *right*, Rupert. The ruined part could be dealt with, and we could grow things — we could be happy here! You'd get better, I'm sure of it — and — and — ' She broke off, not mentioning the secret hope that still lingered in her heart for the child they had always longed for. She was thirty-nine now, true, and they had been married nearly twenty years! Rupert, an architect, retired through ill health, was approaching fifty. But women in more unlikely circumstances had conceived, and she was fit and youthful for her age. Perhaps. 'Well?' she said. 'What do you think?'

The clear pleading gaze of her grey eyes into his decided him. He gave her hand a little squeeze. He was still very much in love with her and guessed the trend of her thoughts.

'We'll see what they're asking,' he said. 'I agree it's picturesque. But a good deal would have to be spent on it.'

They happened to have that 'good deal', and the price, owing to the poor state of the building, was lower than expected and well within the Franklyns' resources.

So they bought Wildgrove.

Builders and decorators were busily employed on the site from spring until autumn mending roofs and chimneys, demolishing what was necessary of the war-damaged wing before converting the rest of that portion to Rupert's plans of a large lounge and conservatory facing the wooded slope.

The couple moved in during late October, the rest of the necessary repairs delayed until the follwing year. This included the high wall of the gardens overlooking the lane below. A few of its stones were fallen or crumbled there, and the main part was thickly entangled and covered by ivy and massed briars, elder, sloes and ferns.

'Let's leave it for the moment,' Elinor suggested. 'It's kind of wild and romantic. The colouring's so lovely too. And I guess there'll be primroses and violets when spring comes.'

Rupert as usual agreed, noting how enthusiasm and excitement in their new home had intensified her natural beauty which was that of nature itself, with her rich copper hair, deep rose-flushed skin, full sensuous lips and everchanging lights of her widely spaced clear eyes.

During their first days following the removal from city to country life and as the certain inevitable physical weariness and reaction wore off, Elinor became aware of a deepening sense of mystery enshrouding the atmosphere. Although comparatively surrounded as the property was by wooded slopes from any high winds, the house and grounds — especially the woods at the back, seemed at times vibrant with an inner unseen life full of whispers and murmurings — of hushed laughter portentous and tremulous with joy.

'Listen,' she said to her husband one day, 'can't you hear it? There are voices too — '

He put a hand to his ear, then shook his head. 'Just that little stream we found,' he said. And after a short pause, 'Are you afraid of gypsies?'

'*Me*? Afraid of gypsies? You're laughing at me. Why would I be? They're colourful. I wouldn't mind at all.' She did not add anything about mysterious shadowy shapes she'd thought she'd glimpsed earlier in the day that certainly had *not* been Romanies — but lighter, without real substance, more delicate and elusive. Rupert after all, despite his poor health, was still just a man who'd laugh off the suggestion as mere imagination. In future she'd keep any strange experiences she had — even if they *were* day-dreams — to herself.

The season was a golden one. Berries shone scarlet and crimson from thick massed bushes where clustered branches bordered the country lanes and gardens. The slopes of Wildgrove were a patterned carpet of yellow, brown, and orange leaves drifted from the woods above.

The weather, mostly still and fine, had the pungent nostalgic smell of distant bonfires, and early mists filmed lawns and vegetation with a glitter of cobwebs.

There was still much to do about the house; Rupert divided hours of every day with odd jobs inside and gardening. A new large greenhouse had been erected for tomatoes, another for vines and a large conservatory planned. The help of a man, Abel Flint, from the village had been arranged. He was well qualified, and a bit of an historian, with a fund of old stories that proved amusing to Rupert. His wife was the postmistress, and his niece, Flora, came daily to help with household chores and give a hand to the woman engaged by Elinor as cook.

'O' course it was different in the old days,' Mrs Flint said to Elinor one morning when she called at the post office. 'In the thirties there was always a dozen or so servants at the hall. That's what they called it then — Wildgrove *Hall*. Footmen and housemaids and two or three men working outside always. But after it was bombed and the poor young mistress died, it was as if the whole heart of the place went too. That's what my old granny told me.' She gave a sigh. 'The war changed everything o' course. Until you and your husband came along no one fancied it.'

'I wonder why.'

'Oh — ' the plump shoulders shrugged. 'Well . . . I s'pose most folk like something more modern now — easy to run, with no sadness lingering about.'

'I find nothing sad anywhere,' Elinor replied promptly. 'We shall have a *lovely* garden when it's properly in order, and the plants so lush. That's one of the things that appealed to me when we found it.'

Naturally she did not add or give any hint of the fervent hope steadily increasing in her day by day that the very richness and earthy vitality of her new surroundings might encourage her to conceive — to blossom as the wild flowering plants and trees thrived there in obeisance to the call and impulses of nature.

Desire deepened in her during those early days at Wildgrove, creating a gentle seduction in her lovemaking with her husband. If he noticed he said nothing; but he marvelled at her renewed happiness that held the quality of a young girl's exuberance, and was irritated at his own failure of complete response.

Sometimes when he was busy in the greenhouse she went wandering alone about the grounds and woods.

It was on a certain late October evening when she was halfway up the slope, that she noticed figures unmistakable this time moving by a group of slender-trunked silver birch. She stood still, interested, and as their forms clarified through the thin rising mist, saw they were those of a man and a woman, with their arms around each other. When they came to a clearing, before cutting from the hill to the other side, they paused, and Elinor saw they were young and clearly in love. He stood with his head bent down to hers. She lifted her face and his lips were on hers in a prolonged kiss.

Everything was very still, holding a mysterious sense of magic that kept Elinor for some moments spellbound. Only a soft flutter of wings as a bird flew from the undergrowth broke the silence. There was a last quiver of clouded radiance from the dying sun and the forms moved and continued on their way to become one with the enveloping shadows of evening.

Elinor didn't attempt to follow them, but turned and returned to the house. Her interest was alerted. She wondered who the couple were, and where they were going.

Nearing the side door of Wildgrove she met Abel coming from the direction of the greenhouse, and stopped him to enquire, wondering if they were neighbours or merely strangers on a stroll; instinct told her they belonged to the area.

Abel stared at her blankly for a second before replying, then shook his head, scratching an ear in a characteristic way he had. 'Those you describe, ma'am, she was wearing a long dress you say, and young? — no, I don't recognize 'em. There's no cottage nearer than Hogget's Farm, an' if they had visitors we'd be knowin'.'

'Oh, I see. Then perhaps they were just looking round, like my husband and I did, when we found Wildgrove.'

He shook his head again. 'I couldn't be sayin', ma'am. Walkers haven't no right to be there anyway. There's no right-o'-way. I'll keep a lookout much as I can, and tell anyone to get off what's private property. We could have a sign put up — a warnin' to trespassers.'

'Oh, no,' Elinor interrupted decisively. 'I hate notices and signboards about. They were doing no harm. I was just interested. They both looked so — happy.'

Abel shrugged and muttered, 'Just as you say.'

And there the matter was dropped.

But not in Elinor's mind.

Following the first intriguing incident she made frequent visits to that particular area of woodland hoping she might see them again.

Three days passed before it happened. November was approaching, and the evening was chilly and grey. Elinor was wearing a long green velvet cape over slacks and a blue sweater. But the woman still emerged as a pale shape through the trees clad in something full-skirted and shimmering slightly giving an impression of a wanderer in the radiance of a moonlit summer night. The man's form was slightly darker. But, as before, they both paused in almost the same spot as formerly, and came together in a romantic embrace.

Enchanted, Elinor moved forward, cautiously, not wishing to disturb them. They appeared to be unaware of her presence and after a minute or so passed on, taking the same route down the slope. During the brief encounter it had been possible to get a clearer view of the girl's face — she was hardly more than a girl — and beautiful. Small-featured and fair, with luminous slightly tilted eyes gazing up to his with such a hunger of love, Elinor's own heart had quickened. Standing there, watching, she'd felt a curious haunting sense of loneliness as their figures passed into the deepening shadows of evening which, for that short time, had been so vibrant with happiness.

Once more the air became empty and chill.

She pulled her cape closer to her chin, turned and made her way back to Wildgrove. She said nothing of this latest encounter to Abel or Rupert, but her bewilderment and curiosity concerning the identity of the couple intensified. In some strange way she felt herself involved, and during the next few days the sensation increased.

In an attempt to divert her mind into different channels she made an effort at tackling physical jobs about the grounds, including a portion of the wall facing the lane where a few bricks had loosened and tumbled through the undergrowth into the weeds and grass.

'Abel can do that,' Rupert said, when he knew, 'or one of the builders in the spring. It isn't women's work.'

'It's mine,' Elinor told him stubbornly. 'Good for my figure. Besides, you never know what might lie buried there.'

Little she guessed then the truth of her prediction.

On a morning when pale watery sunlight, forecast of winter, pierced a thin film of cloud emphasizing the crumbling wall's holes and shadows, she set to work on a tortuous-looking mass not far from the iron gate. Undergrowth had been thickening there for many years. New vegetation and trails of ivy had made considerable impact on tangled branches and dead wood of briar and thorn intermingled with standing weeds, and elder which obviously had been hewn down from time to time.

With tools and fork purloined from Abel's shed, she toiled tirelessly for over an hour and a half, pausing at moments to rest and get her breath back.

And then, quite suddenly, a number of encrusted bricks loosened and fell, sending a shower of soil that left a cloud of dust in the air. Elinor jumped back to escape falling. When she regained her balance and had rubbed her eyes she noticed nothing unusual at first, but as her sight registered saw a cavity in the wall with something curious protruding from it.

She hacked at the soil and dug it out. It was a tin box, green in parts, with a side opening, encrusted and crammed with earth and debris. Puzzled, she bent down to examine the aperture left. Obviously in years gone by it had been contrived and designed as a kind of letterbox. The hole, now thick with clotted earth, had once opened to the road.

Elinor straightened up, forced some of the earth and dust from the lid of the box, and pushed the lid open with the gritty sound of rust crackling.

There was an ancient envelope inside; even as she pulled it out a little cloud of rotten paper fell apart.

She shivered inadvertently, as though a phantom from the past had brushed her skin. A thin rising wind stirred the dead leaves at her feet.

What did it mean?

Faded, spidery-looking writing stared at her as she unfolded the piece of paper. Gone was her previous happiness and concern with the shadowy visitation of the wood. She knew instinctively that whatever lay in her hand was real — a relic of something past and perhaps infinitely tragic.

She didn't work or wait there any longer that day, but went straight back to the house, and after washing herself, settled in a small conservatory she'd made her own, leading from the breakfast room to the garden, and proceeded to examine her find.

The writing, though yellowed and creased was still legible. It was addressed to Guy, and what looked like 'Clavering' with an address to some army depot that was illegible.

Her fingers trembled as she gently pulled the discoloured paper out. Inside the damp covering the writing was clearer. Only one corner was missing.

Automatically, but tense, she started to read.

My dearest love,
Oh, how I missed you when you went away today. I couldn't rest until I somehow got a line to you before you left for wherever it is they're sending you tomorrow with your regiment. I love you so very, very much, so deeply, my darling, life just doesn't seem real without you. This won't be a long letter, because I'm going to leave it in our box for Joseph to collect so that he can catch the earliest post out from the village.

I have wonderful news for you, which is another reason why you simply must take care nothing horrible happens to you. Guess what! Here the next few words were blurred, and the piece missing, but the rest was legible. *So isn't that wonderful? There's no mistake. Doctor Briggs called not long after I'd watched you drive away; he examined me and told me. A baby, darling. Oh, Guy, I'm so very happy, darling. Sad too, of course, that you're*

88

not here. But a sweet sadness — a longing, longing, longing to feel your arms round me, and your body close. How lovely the summer was — those long hours we spent close in the buttercup field near the little wood — nothing ever can spoil or take the memory away. Why did the war have to part us? But it didn't really, did it, love? Whatever happens that time's eternal. And one day you'll come back and we'll be together — with three of us perhaps then. I can hardly believe it. What shall we call the baby? You said Jason, if it's a boy when we talked about the future. Do you remember? But you said, a girl first, if possible. Just like me, you said, with my curly mouth and laughing eyes. Do you remember? And if it is a girl? We thought of all sorts of fancy names, and settled on Anna Rose.

Dearest Guy, I send all my love to you, with a wish — wish — wish across the air for your safety. Perhaps you'll get a leave sooner than you expect, perhaps peace will come quickly and there'll be no more killing. And I shall see you again without your uniform, in your blue shirt coming along the path by the wood.

As ever, my darling,
Lucinda.

Elinor laid the letter down gently on the small conservatory table, and for some moments sat staring through the quiet evening light, motionless, in a kind of dream, shapes of twining plants across the blurred glass roof and windows registered only mechanically on her sight. It seemed for a brief space of time that youthful life from long ago rose and stirred through the silence. The whispered voices and soft laughter, the echo of forgotten footsteps and brush of movement were reborn from the emotional impact of the past.

Slowly she returned to the present, realizing she was cold. Unknowingly, tears had dimmed her eyes.

She understood then; realized the identity of the wanderers through the wood. The deep intuitive hunger in her own being became unified for an interval with the frustrated longing and love of yesterday. Elinor knew, without fully understanding, that she was already deeply involved with the power that was stronger than mortal life or death.

Presently, when warmth had returned, and awareness of her surroundings — the rather shabby sun parlour that her husband was going to repaint, the thick steamy smell of earth and greenery, the little table where the frail piece of paper lay — she forced herself to get up, took the ancient letter in her hand, and discovered one corner had already crumbled. She held the rest carefully and went upstairs to her bedroom. Recently they had had separate rooms sleeping together only when he felt sufficiently fit not to embarrass her. Sometimes — quite frequently — it was a success, and she had forced herself to believe the miracle might happen. Rupert was not old. He only needed Wildgrove and her continued affection and determination to father the child she so desperately desired. If she had felt mildly hurt when he'd suggested taking a smaller room on account of his insomnia and a wish not to keep her awake, she hadn't shown it, but said, 'Of course, if that's what you want. Then when we're together things can be extra special.'

She'd done her very best to keep the flame of passion alight, telling herself he really *did* seem stronger than when they'd first moved into Wildgrove. So the days passed.

But November was intensely cold that year, and Rupert developed a chill. In early November he became seriously ill with 'flu, and despite good nursing and all the doctors could do, pneumonia followed and before the end of the month he was dead.

As soon as that.

Elinor's grief was intense, although at

first — and for weeks following the funeral — she went about in a numbed kind of daze, running the house automatically, breathing, eating, and managing the household without any outward show of grief, refusing at first, with her will, to accept the truth.

Early January came with a sprinkle of snowdrops piercing the brown earth outside and a few Christmas roses that had been planted by her husband earlier in the year.

She began to frequent the woods again: only there did she feel free to let her senses and emotions unwind and the tears fall. But it was not only for Rupert she grieved, but for what they'd been denied — the complete fulfilment and fruit of mutual passion — the joy and laughter and procreation of youth — a little pain perhaps, and bitterness as well as joy — because such lay at the root of all life and in birth itself.

To have *conceived*, and borne the extension of her own being — of herself, and the man she'd married. Now it was impossible.

Or — was it?

The question came in a shock as she stood before her bedroom mirror one day towards the end of January. It seemed for a moment as though a second shape was shadowed behind her. She jerked round.

There was no one there.

Everything was very quiet with the staff below in the kitchen.

A few snowflakes were falling outside, brushing the window as they drifted past the glass. Hardly conscious of what she was doing, she pulled on her cape, went downstairs, and out of a side door, taking the path up to the wood.

Despite the muffled softness of winter the whispering was there again, soft, insistent, rising and falling and changing into little murmurs of pleasure.

She leaned against a birch, the soft blue of her cape blending into the deeper muted blue of the shadows.

And then they came.

Arms entwined as before, wrapt in each other's arms, pausing, sighing, then moving on again. Only this time it was different: instead of going straight down the hill they turned and looked directly at her.

The glow from the girl's eyes — poignant, imploring, was so brilliant, its radiance momentarily seemed to pierce Elinor's heart. She put out a hand and felt a chill at her fingertips, but when she looked down there were only snowflakes there, and the figures were gone.

After that everything was different.

It was as if, in some strange way, Elinor

had absorbed a part of the elusive visitants' identity.

She lived the next few days in a half-dream, enjoying for the first time since Rupert's death the silence and solitary spaces of the old house — not because the quietness was empty, but because of its gentle echoes and sense of unseen stirring life beyond the concept of practical things. Gradually something came alight in her, like the waking of a flower to sunlight.

She was not alone.

It *had* happened.

Definitely.

Miraculous and almost unbelievable as it might seem, she was with child.

When she'd recovered from the shock she took a trip to the village and saw Dr Briggs.

He confirmed what she'd hoped for so long. 'I'm very glad for you, my dear,' he said. 'It will be a late first baby, but you're a strong young woman with a part of your husband now, to share your future with.'

There were a few more conventional remarks and pieces of advice that she accepted in a daze. After the appointment she returned to Wildgrove and informed her cook who had also become something of a friend.

'But tell no one else,' Elinor said. 'A little later maybe we'll get extra help. There'll be a lot to do, and you've more than enough on your plate already. But, it's — it's rather wonderful, isn't it?'

'My dear,' came the kindly reply, 'I'm so very glad for you, that I am.'

Elinor smiled, took the other woman's hand, gave it a little squeeze and said, 'I know. Thanks.'

Then she went out again to the wood.

It was no longer so intensely cold. The suggestion of a thaw was in the air, and a faint rosy glow seemed to tinge the shadows of the chastened trees as she cut up the slope. For some unknown reason she felt it tremendously important that she should contact the wanderers. During the passing of the weeks and past months she had grown to accept their existence as an ethereal reality and not merely as a figment of her own imagination. Never before in her life had she given serious thoughts to ghosts and hauntings. But the circumstances surrounding Wildgrove and her own life had confirmed a growing belief in her that nothing was impossible, and that the elusive couple reflected the identities of the tragic young Claverings. More than that she did not wish to worry over.

The proof of undying love was there. She had material evidence secreted away in her bedroom safe from prying eyes.

The letter.

For more than half a century it had lain in the granite letterbox to be found and cherished for her own comfort following Rupert's death.

A bond.

She found the tree where she usually stood, and waited until they came. But this time it was different; there was a child with them, a very young child, and the forms were more shadowy, although the eyes, when they turned briefly to look at her, seemed more brilliant, like stars against the soft light.

A spasm of delight swept through her. She lifted her arms as though to receive them and took a step forward. But the vision faded; the light died, and the scene was briefly dulled and blank like that of a camera with its lens shut.

Only the shadow of darkened undergrowth remained between the massed branches. Her instant reaction was disappointment — deprivation of her own secret life. But as mobility returned with movement, and full awareness of her surroundings — of a slight breeze rising and rustling the few remaining leaves on the ground, of the stream's trickle and haunting call of a wood pigeon from nearby, she felt a tremendous relief. It was as though any former psychic chains binding her had been suddenly astonishingly released, leaving her free to lead her own physical existence in the world, unhampered by time, past or present, or regrets and grieving for Rupert.

When she reached the house she met Abel coming up the side path with a load of logs.

'May as well get a good supply in,' he said laconically, 'y'can never tell when the weather'll turn cold again.'

'Quite right,' she said.

He gave her a curious look. 'Bin to the wood again, ma'am? The thaw'll make it wet up there.'

'I was just stretching my legs,' she said.

He paused a moment, and loosened the neck of his pullover. 'You seem to like it up there. I prefer the open meself. But when the garden's in proper shape maybe you'll find it more to your fancy.'

'Oh, I shall, don't worry.' She turned in at the side door and found herself saying surprisingly, 'You're quite right, Abel, it is a bit chilly in the wood now. And slippery. I won't be going up nearly so much in future. I'll have other things to think about.'

But she didn't tell him what.

★ ★ ★

The winter months gradually turned to early spring, and Elinor was filled with deep content, spending long hours each day working and making plans for the coming baby. The doctor predicted she could expect it to be born in June but could not say precisely. Neither, looking back, could she work out an exact date. However, she recalled an occasion shortly before his last illness when Rupert had made love to her, and decided she must have conceived then.

She seldom went up to the wood during her pregnancy, but took walks to the village and down the lanes which were starred with celandines, young primroses, and small wild violets.

Sometimes, when the soft spring dusk filled the shadows of the old house, she'd pause and listen to the silence. Like the wood, it was never entirely empty. It seemed to her frequently that Rupert was very near. At other times there'd be the hushed suggestion of gentle whispering and companionship, and she'd fancy a momentary glimpse of a pale face watching. That, of course, was imagination, she reasoned afterwards. There was no one else at Wildgrove but the staff, herself, and the baby she carried.

So time passed. A comparatively easy period for Elinor, considering her age which was then forty. The village had been surprised at the news, outwardly concerned always about her health whenever she appeared, and anxious to be of assistance in any way possible, her having so recently been widowed; but privately commiserating and full of foreboding, Wildbrook being such a strange place.

However, despite dire prophetical and whispered superstitions, the child was born easily without a hitch on a day in June, and was a girl, to Elinor's delight.

She was called Anna-Rose.

★ ★ ★

From her earliest years the little girl proved to be a spirited individual character, sweet-tempered but stubborn. To look at she was slight and fair, unlike either Elinor or Rupert, although the cook insisted that she had her mother's eyes.

'Not really,' Elinor stated. 'The shape widely set perhaps. But the brows — look how they slant. And sometimes the colour changes from grey to almost azure.'

'Oh well, ma'am, you just wait and see. When she's a year or two older the likeness will be stronger. And the way she pokes her little chin up sometimes that's Mr Rupert all over, if you don't mind me saying so.'

Elinor didn't mind at all, but neither did she agree. And, as time passed, the child developed an elusive delicate beauty completely in contrast to the vital, more robust good looks of her mother, or aquiline features of her late father. She was very much her own self, and was also talented. As soon as she was old enough to hold a pencil or brush she was drawing or dabbling with paints, creating strange designs of flowers, trees, and grotesque animals, the products of her own imagination and the countryside — especially the woodlands surrounding Wildgrove.

At six years old Elinor sent her for mornings to a nursery school in the village and later as a day pupil to a girls' school that also catered for boarders. But she was rebellious, and didn't fit in with the rules and regulations, so Elinor took her away and engaged a governess to attend to her education at home.

Miss Pringle appeared to be all that could be desired — youngish middle-aged, well educated, nice looking in a quiet way and even tempered. She quickly grew fond of her young charge and her apparent good manners and sweet smile. By then Anna-Rose was nine years old, and already an accomplished young artist. When she gave her mind to it, she was quick at learning, and preferring the company and gentle discipline of someone she could 'twist round her little finger' rather than obeying scholastic rules and regulations, she made a point of pleasing both her new tutor and her mother.

Two things mildly disturbed Elinor — her daughter's habit of sneaking to the wood unseen on any available opportunity, and her habit of singing to herself when she was alone. Not that the song she hummed was unpleasant — it had a haunting sadness and beauty rising and falling in a minor key that was disturbingly, curiously melancholy.

'Where did you hear that tune, darling?' Elinor asked the child one day.

Anna-Rose's very clear, translucent eyes widened under their delicate fly-away brows. 'Singing? Was I? Oh, I don't know. It's just something — nothing — something I heard somewhere I suppose, perhaps those people.'

'What people?'

'In the wood.'

Elinor's spine tingled. 'They're not supposed to go there.'

'Aren't they? Why?'

'Because it's — it's private property,' Elinor told her, remembering what Abel had said, but annoyed with herself for repeating it after such a while.

'Private?' Anna-Rose laughed. 'Don't be so stuffy, Mummy.'

Elinor's face flushed. 'Don't talk to me like that,' she said unreasonably sharply.

Anna-Rose appeared all innocent surprise. 'Like what? Stuffy? Well, I mean, it *is* stuffy, isn't it — not to want other people sharing things?'

'Oh!' Elinor was confused, and said after a short uncomfortable pause, 'Perhaps so, a bit. But if there are strangers wandering about one's land, I'd like to know who. Tell you what, I'll go with you next time, and then we can both meet them. If they're interested in gardens we could take them round.'

Anna-Rose was not entirely pleased, but she shrugged and said noncommittally, 'If that's what you want.'

The matter was left there temporarily, but a few days later Anna-Rose suggested unexpectedly that they went up that morning. 'Miss Pringle could come too,' she said. 'There are some tiny flowers there I've never seen before. They look like a sort of ever-so-small orchid — I don't know. *Could* they be? Anyway, Pringie wants to see them.'

Elinor laughed. 'Pringie? Is that what you call her? Not very respectful, darling.'

'No. But I'm not a respectful person.'

'That's true,' Elinor agreed. 'You're — ' She paused briefly before concluding, 'I don't know, I'm sure, *what* you are.'

And that was true. Every day that passed, her daughter, who had become so precious to her, seemed to develop some fresh characteristic that intrigued and puzzled her. Perhaps the touch of genius she possessed — or even more than a touch — might account for it, she decided frequently, and found the idea slightly disturbing.

However, on that certain day the three of them, Anna-Rose, herself and Miss Pringle, went up to the wood.

The tiny flowers were there, nestling like small fallen stars in small green clearings. The air was fragrant with the damp earthy smell of waking growing things. Elinor suggested pulling up a clump of buds to plant in the garden or for a pot in the house, but the child disagreed.

'*No*. Leave them. They like it where they are. I shall come up tomorrow and draw some. You can come too, can't you, Miss Pringle? They can be for my nature book.'

It was obvious that Miss Pringle had no

say in the matter. Anna-Rose had already decided.

They wandered about through the trees for a time, an interlude in which Elinor waited hopefully for some sign of 'the people'.

But there was no sign of them, although Elinor had an uneasy sense of unseen company, and at one point when she was resting on a tumbled log, and the other two were examining a plant, she thought she heard a faint echo of Anna-Rose's haunting tune drifting insidiously through the quiet air.

Imagination, she told herself afterwards. There was nothing, no one there. Simply a connection of ideas.

But of what? And what had Anna-Rose to do with any strange former experiences of hers at Wildgrove wood?

Following that unfruitful experience with Miss Pringle and the girl, Elinor deliberately avoided that particular area and occupied herself with business and household matters concerning the estate.

Anna-Rose continued painting and when she was seventeen was already making a name in the art world. A studio was built for her in the garden. Her paintings became known locally. Miss Pringle was still employed at Wildgrove, more as a companion then, and in a secretarial capacity. Soon fame spread, and exhibitions were held in various places. Trips were made to London, enjoyed by the 'original young artist' and her mother, which eventually led to a small but quite important 'forward-looking' gallery accepting her work. There were complimentary reviews but Anna-Rose seemed averse to personal publicity. She enjoyed the creating and recognition of her work, but remained curiously elusive herself, only truly happy in the environment of Wildgrove and the countryside.

Then, shortly after her eighteenth birthday, the mystery occurred which for Elinor was a tragedy.

Anna-Rose disappeared.

The morning had been warm, but with a faint breeze faintly sweet with the drifting scent of bluebells and honeysuckle. She had gone out during the afternoon with her pad and materials, presumably to do some sketching, saying she'd be back early for tea. Elinor didn't worry at first, thinking that as the day was so warm, she'd probably stopped working to relax and possibly dozed off to sleep in the quiet sunshine. But when five o'clock passed, then five-thirty, Miss Pringle, who'd returned from an afternoon's shopping in the town five miles away, went to look for her in the lanes and Elinor made a search of the woods.

There was no sign of Anna-Rose anywhere. Abel said he'd had a glimpse of her shortly after lunch disappearing into the trees, but a little later when he'd gone up to do a bit of felling she'd been nowhere about.

'Of course she may've bin th'other side, ma'am,' he remarked practically. 'I wasn't lookin' f'r her so I can't say. I shouldn't worry if I was you, her likin' a bit of wanderin' now and then.'

But a mist was rising following the heat, and Elinor *did* worry.

She scanned every scrap of forest land she knew, calling, 'Anna-Rose — Anna-Rose — where are you? It's late — come back.' But it was no use, and it seemed to Elinor that the mist itself had an entity whispering the name in her ears with the hushed insidious echo of a sad little tune.

By nightfall, villagers were helping in the search.

The police were informed, and the next day a search was made of any danger spots, including boggy places, old shaft holes, and cliff tracks where there could have been a fall. The press and radio were notified, any gypsy encampments investigated. All to no avail; Anna-Rose had disappeared as effectively as though she'd been swallowed up into thin air.

Time passed. The search for Anna-Rose, listed as a 'missing person', continued. During the first weeks Elinor made continual visits to the wood, hoping against hope for some sign of her daughter. Even 'the people', she thought desperately, whether real or an out-of-the-world experience, might give some clue, because in an unexplainable way she felt they were connected. But there was no sign of them any more. They had vanished as completely as Anna-Rose. If she stood very still sometimes with her face resting against the cool silvery trunk of the birch, as she'd done so frequently in the past, Elinor was aware of a mild haunting, singing sound. But she realized that could have been the wind only, combined with the elements.

Loneliness engulfed her.

For some unknown strange reason she avoided the garden studio. But one early autumn day she took the key and unlocked the door.

A drift of dusty sweet air rushed to meet her.

On the shelves were pots of tiny starry flowers. One or two of the paintings drooped from their hooks on the walls, others were propped up against the wall.

But *all*, she recognized with astonishment, were blank. Either the colours had completely faded or the surface crumbled away.

The next day she made a trip to the small London gallery where Anna-Rose's recent paintings had been sent before her disappearance.

The curator shrugged in negation and told her apologetically, with a note of sympathy in his voice, 'I am so sorry, Mrs Franklyn. About the time of your — of the tragedy — of the young artist's disappearance, her water-colours just faded. It was inexplicable, and very disappointing also. I had a customer who was most anxious to buy one of those very paintings. But as things are' — he shrugged again — 'as it is, nothing can be done. She must have used a very peculiar type of paint.'

'She got them from a local shop,' Elinor said in a daze. 'They looked quite ordinary paints. I'll make enquiries.'

She made a point of calling at the store on her way home to Wildgrove. As she'd expected, the shopkeeper was as mystified as she was.

'I can't understand it,' he said, 'we've never had a complaint from an artist before.'

'Oh, I'm not complaining,' she remarked. 'Perhaps it was something my daughter mixed with it.' But she already sensed that would not be the explanation — that there probably never would be to the strange occurrence. The vanishing water-colours would remain as strange a mystery as the sad little song, the whispering and the quiet shadowy figures of the wood.

She was quite right.

Nothing tangible was ever heard again of anything concerning Anna-Rose. But in time acceptance and a curious sense of peace came to Elinor.

She lived a somewhat reclusive life at Wildgrove, but eventually never felt entirely alone. Much of her time was spent in cultivating a unique wild orchid which later became famed as the Anna-Rose orchid. Her gardens were renowned and open to the public one half day in every week. The woods themselves were kept private, and when she walked there the little song she heard no longer held sadness, but the comforting assurance of enduring love.

She did not attempt to reason logically about what had happened, and when a certain woman visitor one Open Day had the temerity to commiserate with her over the terrible sad loss of her daughter, saying how brave she'd been and how she must have missed her, Elinor replied, 'But she was only on loan to me, you know.'

She smiled benignly, knowing that was true, although the other woman looked mildly affronted, not knowing what on earth she meant.

Elinor Franklyn died in 1970. She was found lying in Wildgrove wood with a bunch of tiny starry flowers in her hand, and on her lips a smile of gentle recognition.

She left no will, so the whole estate of Wildgrove went to her only living relative, a nephew in Canada. He came over and decided to do nothing about it as a year before her death she had sent a letter to him expressing her desire for it to revert to its wild condition as a nature reserve.

Naughty Nellie

Naughty Nellie had been dead forty years when she seduced Leo Crupp.

Leo Crupp was an extremely earnest and learned young man — a professor of archaeology devoted to his subject, pure minded, with little knowledge of the female sex except fleeting gratitude to any of his students who showed proper interest in his lectures, and to his landlady, a buxom, motherly soul who attended to his domestic wants.

Almost half his daily life was spent within the precincts of his university, the rest on tours of research in convenient territories in this country or abroad.

To look at he was tall and bespectacled with a lofty brow and earnest eyes, his features small and finely modelled. There was no way of assessing the inmost thoughts inhabiting that almost noble exterior. The word *almost* has to be applied because at rare moments following an extra glass of wine perhaps — a lapse in the carefully disciplined front might reveal a spark of instinctive frustration betrayed by a sudden

113

high treble of laughter and leap of life in the gentle gaze.

But these brief occasions were rare.

Anyone less likely to attract the attention of a character remotely resembling Naughty Nellie, even in her astral state, could hardly be imagined.

But so it was.

She had probably drifted about the atmosphere so long that her sense of values had suffered, leaving only a wicked sense of humour at the expense of any lurking physical desires.

Whatever the explanation for the following shocking event — it happened.

In this way.

Leo was returning one early evening to his temporary lodgings in St Pennys, following inspection of an ancient site on the moors, when he felt like a snack. Realizing it was later than he'd thought, and his landlady-for-a-week might be annoyed at having to prepare a meal at such an hour, he drew up his small car at a turning where a signpost pointed to the right on which was written WICKENS. TEAS PROVIDED.

The signpost was somewhat the worse for wear, true, but impelled partly by curiosity as to who, if anyone, was still living in such an out-of-the-way spot, he turned up the overgrown lane which, after a bumpy short distance, took another sudden curve, and there it was — a humped cottage in a tangled garden of weeds and bushes behind an iron gate half-broken from its hinges.

Far from disappointment, his interest increased, fanned to life by his passion for antiques.

He drew the car to a halt, and stood briefly staring before making his way to the door. The light was already fading beyond the hills behind him. Everything was very still, and somehow — intimate. He gave a little shudder of pleasant anticipation before knocking on the crumbling paintwork. There was no sound of footsteps or movement from inside, but as he waited a moment or two, the pleasurable thought of home-made scones came to mind.

Obviously the cottage was inhabited; thin shreds of light penetrated the cracks of the building, flickering wanly against the cracked glass of a small window. Being so attuned to the antiquity and general environment of his profession he did not assume, as anyone more logically natured might have done, that it was hardly likely one would find hot scones in such a chilly, deserted habitation, or that a being of Naughty Nellie's calibre might suddenly burst out on him.

He was therefore much shocked, but in a wholly delightful and exciting manner, when the door flew open and there she was — a shining white ethereal vision of bouncing breasts and seductively swelling thighs, with a wreath of phantom posies on her head, and nothing else at all.

Nothing.

She stood there absolutely naked, swinging her plump legs towards him as she had swung them at London audiences from theatrical choruses a century ago.

The substance of her materialization flooded and filled the interior of the broken-down cottage where she'd settled for a brief rest, with an aura of spreading brilliance that exploded in a force of blinding desire, taking Leo Crupp to its very heart.

Any lingering shadow of convention or conscience in him was dispelled and obliterated as he succumbed to the delights of her greedy waking libido, which overshadowed any erstwhile worldly wisdom and ethereal knowledge gathered by her through the years of phantom wandering, drifting about the atmosphere. Her spell was enforced for one specific end — his complete subjugation — in which she succeeded beyond any ghostly hopes. Like most hopes, however, conceived on this mortal planet, its culmination was curiously unrewarding — to Naughty Nellie.

In life she had naturally been used to finales of a more robust calibre in her amours, and the sight of Leo lying open-mouthed and unresponsive on the broken, overgrown paving of the cottage floor was off-putting to say the least. So she drew a whistle of air into her lungs, and drifted to the first available cloud travelling in the direction of the cemetery where she was buried.

The seduction of Leo Crupp was over.

But he never forgot.

Although he apparently recovered from the strange experience followed by the crack on his head which left a nasty lump for a time on his temple, certain harmless peculiarities were noted in his behaviour by his colleagues at intervals. For instance 'scones'. When the word 'scones' was mentioned by his landlady or anyone else, his head would give a quick jerk and a momentary wild flash of interest would light his eyes. For a second only, then it was gone. He also developed a penchant for collecting ancient music-hall programmes, and in his desk wrapped in tissue paper he kept a feminine ribbon garter — relic of the 1880s — picked up, he said, at a sale.

None but himself ever knew the story of

Naughty Nellie and the cottage on the moor. His occasional mildly bewildered mental state was put down to a slight accident with his jalopy on his return journey to his lodgings, following an expedition.

An Odd Affair

This story is not concerned with traditional ghosts or hauntings — or even the occult — directly.

It is just — odd.

And it happened to me personally.

No one could call me specifically an imaginative man, although my work had its romantic side. I am a dealer in antiques and, at times, in the course of business, travel to sales held in various parts of the country.

It was while on one of these occasional jaunts that I discovered Rooksweir in the heart of the West Country, and following a successful business transaction at a nearby historic mansion, decided to stay for a few days at an inn, the Silver Horse, which stood above a green between two wooded hills, overlooking a river. The hamlet itself was scattered closely around, stretching a short way up a slope behind. The effect was picturesque, and the atmosphere strangely peaceful following the stir and constant thrum of city life.

It was nearly midsummer. The fields were green, the air though warm, was fresh and free of the environmental dusts and pollutants which so frequently tainted twentieth-century civilization.

It was late afternoon when I booked in, and the sun cast a rosy glow over the summits of the hills. The landlord and his good lady were both welcoming, placid-looking agreeable people, with gentle voices and broad, smiling faces.

The interior of the hostelry was impeccably clean, furnished in well-polished oak, with a malty smell about that promised good food and ale.

I looked forward to a brief period of complete relaxation and enjoyment of nature, and for two days and nights was not disappointed. I met a few local inhabitants all blessed with the same quality of calm content.

Then, on the third evening, something happened that I have never been able to explain.

I had a dream. Or rather 'a dream' is the logical conclusion, I suppose, to be expected from any rational reader, or listener to my story. That the night in question happened to be Midsummer's Eve must be purely coincidental.

I'd had an easy day of resting and taking gentle walks through winding lanes and along hill paths, and after a satisfying meal followed by a drink in the bar of one of the landlord's wife's special home-brewed wines, felt ready for an early night.

'You'll not be going to the celebrations, surr, then?' Mrs Jolly asked, brows raised above her pink, apple face. 'But, no, perhaps it wouldn't be your kind of fun, being a city gentleman.'

'What happens?' I enquired. 'Bonfires?'

'Oh, that's not all,' she said. 'Fun and games like.'

Feeling I'd had enough exertion and not really in the mood for anything resembling a carnival, I told her I'd think about it. I had already thought, of course, and decided in the negative, intending to have a good night's sleep as my plan was to leave for town next morning, having received a telegram earlier in the day concerning business.

I hoped the 'celebrations' would not be too disturbing.

They were.

But in a very peculiar manner.

The sunset was rosy, leaving still a faint glow in the sky when I went to bed, but once there, being healthily tired and with the soft air cool on my face from the open window, I was soon asleep.

The first tinkle of a bell, followed by what

sounded like the thin sounds of a fiddle, woke me with a start. I lay for some moments puzzled, then recalled what I'd heard earlier of the planned celebrations.

I got up and went to the window and pulled the curtains aside. There was a moon rising, clarifying a number of chattering, gyrating figures already jogging about in some kind of formal dance on the green below. Others, with waving arms, were appearing from different directions from the hillside paths. There was laughter and singing, bowing and gesticulating, while the thin strains of the fiddle whined and moaned with the sounds of a rising summer wind.

I sensed nothing extraordinary about the scene at first. Just a company of country people enjoying some sort of traditional ceremony, I thought.

And then, gradually, as my sight and senses registered more clearly, I knew I was wrong. A number of the revellers were not human at all. There were few if any in the little crowd, most resembled animals attired in festive clothes, including a cow, a pig, a sheep and a fox who was the fiddler. There were others, and the atmosphere was electric, exuding a weird joyousness that made me wish for a moment to join them. I was on the point of dressing when the fascination turned to a kind of atavistic fear.

You will say, of course, that I was dreaming, or half asleep or that the whole event was an illusion due to my mood and the half light, and partly perhaps to Mrs Jolly's homebrewed wine.

Quite a natural conclusion, but in this case not entirely correct; in fact one odd feature about it remains a mystery to this day, though an historic book of legends concerning the district provides a possible theory together with my own deductions.

Anyway, I had no more sleep until the first glimmer of dawn but watched intermittently the distorted ballet of shadows and contorted shapes to its final scene against the hillside when, one by one, the frollickers dispersed and disappeared along their different routes in the grey cloak of morning mist.

The wailing, singing and music ceased.

The sighing wind died to calm.

All was still — weirdly quiet. I crept to my bed and had two hours' slumber.

When I woke it was to the normal sounds of the countryside and inn life; the rattle of a milk churn, a man's whistle, clatter of feet below and all normal signs of breakfast ahead.

I got up and dressed and went down to the bar parlour having decided to stay another day and night, to make a certain investigation.

Mrs Jolly had her usual dreaming smile when I appeared.

'Good morning, surr,' she said, 'and did you have a good night through all the village jollifications?'

'As good as could be expected,' I replied. 'I saw a good deal from the window. Most interesting. Especially the music — and the masks.'

'Masks, surr? Oh, there were no masks. We don't use masks for *that* occasion. Midsummer. No need.'

'But the animal heads? And the costumes — ?'

'The costumes are natural for the event. Generally the public keep away. They're not interested. And, of course,' — she paused with a twinkle in her eye — 'my special brew can be quite potent. Animal heads you say? Well, now, aren't we all related to the dear dear things in some kind of way?' She gave a hearty laugh.

'I've never thought about such a thing from that angle,' I told her. 'Darwinian theories aren't exactly in my line.'

'Oh, this has nothing to do with Darwin,' she said promptly. 'Rooksweir folk have their own origins and traditions.'

The remark struck me as having far more

behind it than was immediately apparent, and enforced my decision to prolong my stay at the Silver Horse a little longer. My business in town could wait.

So I told Mrs Jolly, and the booking was arranged.

That morning I drove to the nearest town twenty miles away, and paid a visit to the local library which proved to have quite an extensive reference section dealing with West Country areas. I spent two hours thumbing through volumes of both historic and legendary details, and at last in a yellowed, calf-bound edition found a page I wanted.

Under ROOKSWEIR in large type was a second one in smaller print saying 'Facts and Fiction', and below a full page concerning the vicinity.

I drew up a chair to a long table in the centre of the room, and began to peruse the information.

'In the sixteenth century', it read, 'a certain squire of Rooksweir reputed to be an eccentric recluse, preferring the company of animals to his own human kind, did cut himself off from normal company to devote his whole life and interests to that of four-legged creatures both of the wild and domestic varieties, living in close kinship with all. Except for two devoted servants he did shun the human race and was likewise avoided by local inhabitants, being said to be insane. Certain nights of each year were put aside for quaint carousing and celebrations, including Midsummer Eve when all of his strange company did dance together and make merry. For many years following his demise this squire who did become known as 'Mad Mullins' was said to haunt the hills of Rooksweir with his strange clan.

'Music and wild sounds could be heard when the moon was right, and macabre dancing shapes patterned the hills the like of which have never been seen before or since.

'In this year of 1750, Rooksweir is avoided by both local folk and strangers who had heard of such unholy goings on at that particular time of year.

'No doubt in the far future the event will become established as a legend.

'The squire's mansion which at one time housed such strange company was converted and rebuilt at a later date, and is now the site of an inn, the Silver Horse.'

Well, I thought; here was something to go upon. A mere legend? But the source must have arisen from some kind of fact, although how much I intended to discover as accurately as possible.

I did not spend any more time in the library, but got back to Rooksweir as soon as I was able, and after a quick lunch set about my enquiries, calling first on the village cleric, Pastor Black.

He was a short, dark, brown-faced, rather aggressive gentleman who seemed at first resentful at being in any way questioned over the village inhabitants. 'Their spiritual well-being is my concern,' he said, 'and I would not agree to divulge *any* confidential matters which are entirely *their* affair and mine.' He spoke defiantly, reminding me briefly of a bulldog about to bare his teeth, but I managed satisfactorily, with a certain amount of guile and flattery, to soothe him down, and after such reprehensible behaviour on my part, succeeded in gleaning the names of the local families — Bullock, Fox and Lamb. Mrs Bullock was the postmistress, Mr Fox the schoolmaster, and Mr Lamb a carpenter. There was also a Mrs Cowley, and a Ramsey.

'All very admirable people,' he said smugly, 'and members of my flock. If they were involved in any celebrations on *any* evening, I can assure you it was purely innocent fun.' He regarded me challengingly over his spectacles.

'Of course,' I answered in like vein. 'I wouldn't dream of suggesting otherwise.'

He appeared appeased, and went on to compare the sins of modern commercial life with the virtues of his own rural community.

We parted on apparently amicable terms, despite the lingering suspicion in his small beady eyes, and I continued my round of social calls, with the excuse of gathering data for the writing of a country novel.

I visited Mrs Bullock first. She was an innocent-looking rather large woman who obligingly supplied me with details of the flora and fauna of the district, but on other matters — social activities — was less forthcoming. However, before I left her I gleaned another interesting name of a resident — Mr Hare.

Eventually, after tramping round the area for over two hours, and through devious means, I had collected quite eight names of local inhabitants, all being references to various animals.

My last port of call was at the schoolhouse, following the afternoon's lessons. During conversation I referred lightly to the 'interesting occasion' of Midsummer Eve. William Fox had a pointed face and small eyes with a crafty look in them; I would not have fancied being his pupil.

'Animals,' he said, '*dancing*? Oh, that is just nonsense, sir. Some of the local people like a few games at such a time and trip-a-toe at Sir Roger de Coverley — whatever else you thought you saw, was just imagination, sir. No more. *Imagination.*'

That was all.

But yet — not quite.

Although I pretended to be satisfied, I wasn't.

When I stared at him closely I could perceive a wisp of red hair sticking to his chin. Was it beard? — or *fur*? And his ears *were* really somewhat pointed.

There can be no conclusive answer. But I think you'll agree that the whole episode *was* an extremely *Odd Affair*, and *could* have links with the past.

The Traveller

The building loomed at first as a mere blurred shadow against the fog. Then, as he drew nearer, lungs choked by the cloying damp air, walls took shape with a hazy pattern of windows and darker doorway. There was a creaking and a sudden stream of water against his face — obviously from a signpost in the wind, and a blurred sliver of light zig-zagging in a crooked line over the ground to meet him. His immediate reaction was to thank God for some sign of human habitation after wandering about the moor. With luck — and he'd not had any till now since setting out on his holiday in escape from the rat race of city life — he would find some sort of shelter till the weather cleared.

He must have been blundering about lost in the wilderness for hours, heaven knew how many. He felt numbed, chilled with the wet and cold. His torch had failed, his last cigarette and matches gone. So any refuge, however primitive, would be welcome. Perhaps even life saving. If he'd had an inkling how swiftly fog could descend without warning he'd certainly never have set out in the first place.

Three strides more and he was there. The door was slightly ajar; he pushed it and went in.

There was no hall, just a dimly lit interior with a lamp at the far end, a couple of benches and a raised counter. Obviously a bar.

Everything was very silent, muffled as though any company there had been numbed to weird communion with the elements.

He rubbed his eyes and stood staring, perceiving after a moment or two glimmers of transient light in one corner which evolved into a number of bald heads grouped around a table. At the same time there was a tinkle from the counter and, turning, he saw the lamp move and a male figure emerge elongated to a thin column of darkness against the slightly pale background. A second shape, female, broad and squat with a wild moon face under massed reddish hair, followed from behind. She came to the forefront and lifted a plump beckoning finger.

'What you want?' she creaked, in a voice with the squeaky inflection of the whining wind. 'Who're you? Friend or foe?'

The traveller moved forward. In his

bewildered numbed state it seemed that the faces under the white, bald heads at the corner table were all lifted towards him. They were blank, yet holding a frozen immobility of expression that was frightening.

'I'm — I'm lost,' he said. 'I saw your light and thought perhaps you might have shelter for me and food.' His voice died in his throat.

'Oh, ais! There's plenty o' shelter 'ere.' She laughed and her laugh might have been the shriek of an angry gull. 'Here they come, all o' them, one by one from the tomb they come — '

He shuddered and turned for escape into the wet dark, away from the horrifying place, but was prevented by a nightmarish company of cowled grey figures with gaping jaws and empty eyes, an evil force of decay baleful to human life.

The wanderer, defenceless, staggered back smothered by the lusting sea of risen dead. His last moment of awareness was of the woman's moon face, looming above him and white-boned fingers pressing a goblet to his mouth.

'No — ' he protested weakly. 'No — ' But it was too late. Liquid, ice cold, with a faintly bitter-sweet odour, trickled down his throat and then darkness mercifully claimed him.

He fell.

Dawn was lighting the sky when the wanderer's body was found by a passing farmer near a heap of tumbled stones — the relics of an ancient ruin — a short distance away from a lonely hamlet crouched in a fold of the moors. Nearby, a long-deserted church and graveyard frequented only by sheep and wild creatures, stood stark with twisted spire and cold tombstones, mostly half fallen above the dark damp earth.

Later, death from exposure and shock of some kind was given at the inquest on the victim.

'It was shock all right,' one local inhabitant said to another. 'No one in his senses should've taken to visiting that place on All Souls' Night. But then maybe he didn't know.'

'P'raps he *did*,' his companion suggested thoughtfully. 'He could've bin one of they investigatin' sort of fellow — you know, the psychic sort, don't they call 'em? Come to check up on old history. Jane Barrows at the village library says she gets 'em from time to time lookin' up old books and records of legends, an' what happened in the past round about?'

'Checkin' up you mean?'

'Somethin' like et. Not that I b'lieve in a lump of old stones bein' haunted. Not *actually*. Seems to me all balderdash. Still — '

'Best to be on the safe side, *I* say. There was the inn all right, we *do* know that, and a bad place it was when it was standin'. An' say what you like, evil such as *her* kind — Alice Potts and that man o' hers, Obadiah — takes a lot o' properly killing. How many do they say was murdered and lies buried now in the graveyard there by the church?'

'Twenty or so known; but only the Devil knows how many more she poisoned and got away with, an' all for greed. All travellers, all rich an' lost. The smuggling too. A little gang of them there was, an' a crooked priest to take his share of the spoils.'

'Hm. Still, that was long enough ago. Three hundred years they do say. You can't believe all you read about from times so long ago.'

'It makes no difference anyways, not to that poor man now — he's gone, and it's the last we'll hear of him, I reckon.'

But this was not quite the case, of course. References were later made in the Press further afield, to a certain Doctor Richard Maybury, celebrated historian and author of books dealing with British legends, who had died from exposure and cold while on a walking tour of the Cornish moors.

It is ironic, one report ran, *that Doctor Maybury should have met his death on All Souls' Night near the exact spot where the ill-famed inn* The Golden Egg *once stood, run by the mass murderers, Alice and Obadiah Potts, who first poisoned their victims before robbing them and burning their bodies.*

The site is reported by local inhabitants to be haunted.

The River

Rupert Carne had always been fascinated by the picture. It had been painted by an uncle of his, John Carlton, as a young man when the boy was only eight years old.

Rupert remembered him as a sensitive, delicate character, living alone with his mother at Marshlands, a remote house on the east coast. For a few years the boy was sent there for summer holidays to enjoy paddling about the small pools with his shrimping net, and building sand castles on the long pale beach. Small yellow daisy flowers grew about the dunes, and on clear days tiny blue butterflies glinted in the sunlight.

John was a gifted artist although he had not sufficient strength to work for long at a time. Shortly before his death he had an exhibition which was praised by the critics who agreed he had a 'brilliant future before him'. An ironical statement, under the circumstances.

The painting referred to at the beginning of this story had earned high acclaim which was why his mother kept it. This fact, of

143

course, meant nothing to Rupert who was too young to appreciate verbal praise.

He just liked it, because it set his imagination alight in a strange subtle way.

It represented nothing vivid or colourful, showing merely — although 'merely' perhaps is an inadequate word to use — a river winding between misted hills and finally disappearing around shrouded banks to its unknown end.

On Rupert's rare visits to Marshlands before his great-aunt too died, he became further obsessed by the scene. The painting hung in a recess of a room that had been his uncle's study. A low-bulbed light had been conveniently placed to give the vista a subtle luminosity and effect of ethereal life, and he would stand for minutes at a time staring, and wondering.

Wondering what lay behind the bend. At times, even, he fancied a quiver of movement stirred the silvered thread of distant water. Where did it lead? What presence or secret territory waited hidden behind the humped hills under the fading sky?

His family kept the property, using it for brief respites from town and for holidays. The painting was never removed and it retained its fascination for Rupert. When he inherited the house for himself he was a man of fifty, and he retired early for health reasons after deciding to leave town and make Marshlands his home.

He had never married; perhaps if he'd had a wife and children to think about things might have worked out differently. As it was, although he enjoyed his freedom from business and the rat-race of city existence, he became increasingly aware at intervals of a certain loneliness and lack of purpose. He did not make friends easily, and except for visits to the local pub at Hungersly, the nearby village, he had little contact with humanity. His housekeeper, an elderly family retainer, was aware of this.

'Why don't you join the golf club, Mr Rupert?' she asked him. 'It's only a mile from here, and you used to enjoy a round once. The company and exercise would do you good. You look a bit lost sometimes. Wisht! Get the colour back into your cheeks.'

He smiled and shook his head. 'I'm all right, Mrs Cox. I enjoy walking on my own.'

'Living in the past you are,' she said a trifle sharply. 'Childhood memories, and thinking of your uncle. No good looking back. It's the present and the future that matter.'

'Oh, I don't think of Uncle John — at least only occasionally,' he answered, and this was

145

true. He hadn't known him well, and time between them had been brief. It was still only the painting that haunted him.

During the first summer months following his final return to the old house, he made an effort to shake off the obsession by exploring parts of the country district he'd not known before. He did a little fishing, and drove occasionally in his small car to the nearest town library ten miles away where he studied books on the history of the district. But such diversions from his preoccupation with the painting were only temporary, fading as soon as he entered the house again, and when autumn came, bringing yellow heavy skies and cold mists to the land and sea, his introspection increased, awakening all his former curiosity concerning the picture.

He spent hours at a time in the study with the excuse to his housekeeper that he was dealing with old papers and letters, and was thinking of writing a book about his uncle's short life.

He forced himself into half-believing such was true. But *she* knew, and so did he, secretly, that it wasn't. The scribbled notes concerning dates and certain minor events were all pretence. In reality his mind was obsessed by one thing.

The painting.

He grew thinner.

As time passed his appearance deteriorated; there were occasions, following the midday meal, after retiring to the small room, when, in a half-dazed state, he felt himself receding into the pictured scene. He imagined walking along the path bordering the shining water, and walking under the humped line of hills to its destined end.

When he pulled himself back to full consciousness he felt drained, exhausted by the effort.

Although he took little notice of his housekeeper's admonishments, she continued with her reasoning.

'Wouldn't it be pleasanter for you to use the studio upstairs?' she queried. 'There are a number of his pictures there, and it's a nicer room, more airy. I could make a nice fire for you, and you'd have a view of the sands and sea — ' She broke off as he shook his head.

'I'm comfortable in the study, Mrs Cox. The atmosphere's right for me. Please don't worry. There's nothing wrong. I shall get more colour back when spring arrives again.'

But with spring matters grew worse.

The weather became brighter, with a sharpness that seemed to penetrate to the interior of Marshlands. Outside, sometimes there were days of glassy clarity giving brilliance to sea and sky, striking in a vivid shaft of light through the window in the study so the picture assumed a startling life of its own.

Rupert was having his usual siesta one day when something happened.

He roused from a half-sleep to find himself standing up. He stretched out an arm and to his astonishment the canvas seemed to melt at his touch. He felt only a gentle brush of air as his fingers reached towards the sky and, when he moved forward, there was faint movement of the water. A damp mingled smell of moorland and river scent filled his nostrils; he peered more closely and glimpsed around a bend in the scene. For some moments he remained transfixed, then everything darkened. He staggered back to his chair. His heart was thumping as his blurred eyes gradually cleared. When sight fully registered, the picture appeared as it had always been.

He said nothing, naturally, of his strange experience to Mrs Cox, trying to convince himself the whole episode had been an illusion — a fantasy from a dream. For a few days he deliberately went out more, and tried to enjoy a chat at the village pub with the few acquaintances he'd made. At first the effort seemed to be working; he had less opportunity of becoming involved with his obsession.

Mrs Cox remarked that he was looking better. 'I don't suppose you meet any nice young ladies there?' she queried one evening on his return to the house. 'But it would be pleasant for you to have a bit of feminine company now and then.'

She glanced at him hopefully.

With a hint of acerbity he replied, 'I'm not in need of any woman fussing about me,' adding politely, 'except you, of course. You do all that's necessary for me.'

'Ah. But I shan't be here always, Mr Rupert. And — it was other things I was thinking of.'

'I know. And please don't.'

He turned away.

His brief experience with the feminine sex while he was in town had been unfortunate. On the few occasions approaching any intimacy he'd been badly disappointed.

He was a perfectionist. And he'd never yet contacted any girl or woman even remotely resembling the exquisite vision required to hold his interest.

So, inevitably, when the weather changed again and became wet, his deeply rooted obsession with the painting returned. More than ever the curling line of water and pathway assumed its insidious beckoning quality, haunting his senses with a whispering magnetism urging an exploration of its mysterious territory.

'Find out for yourself,' the message urged. 'You can if you really want to. Wish — wish — and dream. Dream. Let yourself drift — '

Outwardly he made a stern effort to appear normal before Mrs Cox. After all, while he could eat, live, and converse with ordinary human beings he was not mad. There's nothing peculiar about you, he told himself many times when viewing his appearance through the mirror. It's just that you have an appreciation of Uncle John's work more than anyone else.

He made various enquiries from art experts and owners of galleries concerning the locality of the river scene, but with no success. The painting *could* be just a product of its artist's imagination, he decided logically. But this line of reasoning made no difference. Whoever painted it, wherever it was — the picture *lived*.

And the knowledge somehow was awesome and rather frightening.

A day came when rain fell heavily in a monotonous regular drip of sound against the dreary walls and windows of the house.

Rupert, imprisoned by the isolation, had no desire to escape except through means of the painting. He'd lost his appetite, and retired earlier than usual for his siesta in the study. Mrs Cox was worried. She forgot herself, lost her temper and said sharply, as he passed up the hall, 'You take too much notice of that old painting. I've half a mind one day to get rid of it sometime when you're not about. 'Tisn't natural.'

He stopped short and faced her with such rage on his face and wildness in his expression she flinched. 'If you did,' he told her in deathly flat tones, 'I'd kill you.'

Frightened, she turned away, determining to try and get a doctor to see him.

But she didn't have a chance.

After that unpleasant confrontation he settled himself as usual in the study, fixed his gaze on the well-known scene, and waited.

Gradually the precinct and surrounding everyday furnishings of the room faded becoming a blurred misty vacuum of greyish air. He pulled himself to his feet, and the vista widened and changed until he found himself moving shakily forward into it. Once his feet touched the damp turf his stance steadied, and he could smell more pungently this time, the moist water scent of the silver thread of river flowing beside him. A sense of excitement flooded his being. He was there at last, was making his way towards its first loop and as he rounded the bend a further line of misted distant hills came into view. There was one more curve threading to the left behind a mysterious dimmed stretch of rising land, and he *knew* — sensed instinctively — that there lay the key and answer to his existence: the vision of perfection that had haunted his inmost soul for most of his life.

He pressed on, drawing the breath deeply into his lungs, feeling himself a pilgrim to an unknown shrine. He could not visualize her; he never doubted her feminine presence. She would hold the purity of a spirit and the beauty of Aphrodite. This — this was the answer to all he'd waited and longed for during his adolescent and adult years. His uncle's work was merely a symbol of it — his message perhaps, conveyed in paint.

But the reality was no painting, it was — eternity.

He stumbled slightly as he turned the corner, then recovered his balance and stood magnetized.

She was there!

A graceful bowed figure seated on a rock, with her head half-bowed on her lily slim neck, slightly turned away from him. She was wearing something flimsy that had a translucent ethereal quality, almost radiant. Its soft folds clung to the slim lines of breasts and thighs seductively.

Oh, she was beautiful. All he'd ever wanted and never thought to find.

And he knew she was his. He would not have to fret over the painting any more. Its precious secret was at last revealed.

He moved forward more quickly. The lowering clouds over the hills and river lifted as she looked up and turned her head to face him. The gauzy scarf flowing loosely over her hair fell back.

Her face was clear.

And then, with a stab of horror, he saw. The eyes staring at him bleakly were mere empty slits, and cold.

Dead eyes.

The mouth, whose kisses he'd anticipated, was a thin hard line. No tinge of colour stirred the stretched skin of her cheekbones. When she opened her arms to him they were mechanical and held no welcome. It was death, not life, facing him.

With a gasp of terror he turned to make an effort to retrace his steps. But it was no use. Her grip was already upon him, and when he tried to fight his way back through the terrain of the painting the air had thickened and become a barrier of crumbling,

153

cloying material used by his Uncle John half a century ago.

He was found later by Mrs Cox lying on the study floor, with the tumbled, broken picture over him. His death was said by the authorities later to be from a massive heart attack. But privately the housekeeper confided to a friend, 'He'd been an ill man for many, many years. If you ask me he'd inherited something sick from his uncle. Can you inherit that kind of sickness? I don't know. But I never liked that painting. It had something funny about it.'

A True Story

I first saw the squat figure when I was a baby lying in my cot, staring at the pattern of shadows on curtains and wall, and she was there! — hunched and dark — in a corner of the room; a malevolent-looking creature with the appearance of some grotesque giant frog or black pug-dog, watching me.

I was terrified.

I remember I screamed. But she never stirred, just continued looking at me. A nurse came to comfort me. In the end my father must have been called. He put his hand through the frightening creature to show there was nothing there and that the apparition was merely a shadow.

But when he'd gone she was still sitting in the same place.

What happened eventually I don't remember. Perhaps I was taken to another room. But through my babyhood and very young childhood I was haunted intermittently by the presence of the ugly dwarf-like thing.

I never liked sleeping alone through those very early years. Until my younger sister was born, going to bed at nights was secretly frightening. Always when my mother came to say goodnight I'd ask her if they were going out that evening. On those occasions, of course, there was always a nurse or maid about somewhere. But that made no difference, the fear remained. At such times after my parents left the house to go to parties or the theatre, I'd creep out of bed if I had the chance, unseen, to the top of the stairs from where the front door was visible at the end of the hall below, and sit there shivering, waiting for the sound of my father's key in the lock in the door and the sight of it opening, revealing the two familiar figures. My father in his top hat and my mother with the funny boa thing around her neck.

In later years the terror receded, but there was a sequel.

When I was almost grown-up, my grandfather, whom I adored, told me he used to see some little black hunched form during his early childhood.

So?

What is the answer?

I have never been quite able to find a logical explanation.

Shall I ever see her again?

I sincerely hope not.

The Window

I had been living only a month at Treeshill following my retirement from town life, when I noticed the house.

I'm not a good sleeper; I suppose you could call me an insomniac, and possibly the extreme quietness and sudden solitude — Treeshill is a very remote district in the West Country — had made me more than ever vulnerable to night thoughts and impressions. Anyway, I was wandering round my new property about two o'clock, an hour when most sensible people are in bed, when it happened.

My cottage stood on a hill, overlooking a valley that rose on the other side in a sharp slope of moorland to a further rim of hills, almost mountains. The weather had been thundery — which could partially explain my particular restlessness on that certain night, but rain hadn't fallen, and when I looked out from my bedroom the sky was clearing sufficiently to show a thin crescent moon breaking through cloud. I was about to turn away, and then stopped, startled to see on the opposite slope a square of window brilliantly lit, illuminating the scene for several seconds, or perhaps a full minute. At the same time the dark shape of a large building emerged in the background. But more compelling still the outline of a woman seated behind the window riveted my attention.

She was brushing her hair — long hair that caught passing flickers of light on it — with slow rhythmical strokes, and almost instantaneously a man entered and bent down to kiss her shoulder.

Although out-of-date now to admit myself a romantic, I suppose fundamentally I always have been — secretly, and just for that short interim the little scene stirred me poignantly. I tried to look away, but was unable to do so. In any case there was no need. Just as quickly as it had appeared, the square of light was switched off, and all was dimmed into darkness.

Gone.

The woman — or girl, whichever she was — and the man, the massive surrounding setting of the large house, which could have been a small mansion, had disappeared into the general darkness.

Disappointed at the sudden finale, and also puzzled, I made my way back to bed, aware of something lost that I might never find again. But, of course, that line of reasoning was absurd. There *had* been a house, and there were human beings living there, I'd had proof. What caused my bewilderment was that on the two occasions when I'd walked that way in the daytime, I'd seen no building of that type visible — only a fairly modern converted small house, and a farm quite a mile away.

The next day it rained so I didn't walk as I'd intended to make a further inspection of the land across the valley, but occupied myself with a few business and domestic matters which included the unpleasant task of writing to my estranged wife finalizing my plans for divorce. The matter had been one of my main reasons for leaving London. For months we'd been separated following her affair with a married man who at one time had been my best friend, which made things so much worse. The discovery had been a particularly unsavoury business. Oh, she'd wanted to patch things up. The involvement had been short, and I'd known she regretted it. But the whole thing had been too much for me.

I was never one for second best.

So there it was.

Finished.

I suppose if I'd tried hard enough I could have found excuses for her. My work as surveyor had taken me away a good deal. But before she'd married me she knew how things were. Perhaps if we'd had children — but eight years had passed without any. I didn't particularly want kids during that time, and she didn't seem to care. I'd taken it for granted we were sufficient for each other.

Obviously I'd been wrong.

So I'd taken the only course possible, hadn't I?

In spite of my determination to wipe the misalliance clear from my mind, the questioning returned constantly during that long wet day at Treeshill. Until the evening, the heavy rain continued, then, about six o'clock the sky lightened. A wind rose from the north dispersing the massed clouds and by evening it was fine.

And that night I saw it again.

The window.

I managed to sleep from eleven to one-thirty. But once awake I knew I wouldn't drop off again for some time. So I got up, wandered about a bit, wondering whether to take a tot of whisky or not, and decided on the latter.

I pulled the curtains of my window wide and looked out. Except for a few stars all was shadowed darkly. Then, suddenly, there was a flash of light. I blinked and a second later it was there — a shining square of golden light on the opposite hill, with the woman's figure as before outlined intriguingly like some legendary figure from a fairy-tale — brushing her hair.

I didn't move but stood magnetized until the male figure appeared and went through the similar procedure as the first time, bending his head to her shoulder.

Like watching the scene from a play I waited for the next move, but there was none. The square went blank, absorbed by a crumbling of the house itself into a ferment of thickening cloud.

Rain was coming. A faint rumbling of the elements suggested approaching thunder.

I lingered about for some time restlessly, wondering if the illusion, mirage, apparition, or actual panoramic physical happening would be repeated, but nothing more appeared.

Until morning all remained dark and blank. The night withheld its secrets.

The next day was fine. I set out early, determined to discover the truth concerning what I'd seen. In the light of day logical argument was more easy. I hadn't been dreaming, I knew that. There must be a large house somewhere in the vicinity where the lighted window had appeared. That I'd witnessed the sentimental episode concerning the girl brushing her hair at almost precisely the same hour on two separate nights *could* have been coincidence. That I'd failed to notice the building on my previous rambles on the opposite hill could have been a mere trick of geography. Moorland hills and mountains could be misleading. What had been seen from my window could have been hidden naturally when viewed from certain angles, by a possible fold in the land or rock formation.

Such arguments were uppermost in my mind when I reached the smallish house I'd noted formerly standing precisely in its square of garden where I'd judged the 'house of the window' to be.

It stood on its own, with no other building in view except a corner of the farm, and had probably been built in the late forties or early fifties when new homes had been in demand following the war. A very ordinary conventional small house with a square of garden in front bordered by a tidily kept hedge.

I decided to take the chance of receiving a rebuff to my enquiries, and gave a rap on the door knocker.

It was some moments before I had a

response. Then I heard the yap-yap of a dog followed by the tap of a stick and footsteps.

There was a creaking of wood on tiles, and the door opened cautiously. The head of a very old lady poked out. Her sight was obviously poor. But although she wore glasses the eyes squinted above them, and her voice was gruff when she queried, 'Yes? Who are you?'

Knowing I had to act warily I did my best to put her at her ease, and when I'd explained carefully it was simply help in locating the building I'd witnessed from across the valley, she invited me inside to her sitting-room.

It was a conventional, comfortable interior, reminiscent of the early thirties or late twenties, with china ornaments on the mantelshelf above the glimmer of a small coal fire. Pink curtains hung at either side of the window which was draped by thin lace, and a cuckoo-clock ticked on the wall nearest the door.

She directed me to a high-backed easy chair and motioned with her stick.

'Sit down, sir. These old legs of mine prefer resting to standing up nowadays.' And when I'd done so, and she was comfortably seated herself, she continued, 'You were asking about a large house — a mansion you say? Well, I can help you in one way, but not in the way you want, I'm afraid. There's no building of that kind anywhere near here.' She shook her old head firmly. 'I can assure you that is true. Whatever you saw or *thought* you saw — it was no *house*. The farm — Ballans Farm — is the only habitable building on this part of the moor for many miles round.'

'But the silhouette was quite clear,' I persisted, 'and each time the girl was brushing her hair. And then the man came in. It was somehow — very poignant.'

I waited. For seconds she didn't move. Everything suddenly seemed very still. It was as though time had stopped and her eyes were concentrated on something I couldn't see, a world unknown to me. The only movement or murmur in that small quiet room was the tick-tock of the cuckoo-clock.

Then she spoke in a voice grown tired from age. 'You must be one of the few, then.'

'I don't see — '

She interrupted me with a sharp tap of her stick on the floor. There was a crackle of the fire, and the sudden chiming of the clock at the half-hour.

'Cuckoo — cuckoo — '

'Yes. One of the few,' she echoed. 'From

time to time it *has* happened, but very rarely. Oh, only once, no, twice, since this house was built nearly fifty years ago.'

Knowing I was about to learn something if I didn't interrupt her narrative, I waited for what she had to tell — until her story was resumed.

'Once upon a time,' she commenced, as though starting a fairy-tale, 'there was a house here, as you describe, a large house. Fairwood Hall they called it, on this very spot.' She drew a breath that was more of a sigh — a sigh of regret. 'This one, *my* house, was built years later, and I took it. It seemed fitting somehow, and right. You see — in my time — when I was young, I was employed as nursemaid by the family who owned it.'

'I see.'

She shook her head. 'No, you don't, my dear, no one does — not the full truth of it. Only the sadness, and that's just history now. History's written and read. But the pain of it's only felt by any who *knew* and lived it.' She paused. I could sense her mind wandering through the years, and dared not question her until the life returned to her eyes again. Then I questioned gently, 'Won't you tell me the rest?'

She jerked her head up with a little start.

'After what you saw — *thought* you saw — maybe I should say. I was very fond of that family as you'll have gathered. Miss Rosalind in particular. And her young fellow — her fiancé — was a fine young man. They'd been married that day — the day of the tragedy, and it was planned for them to go abroad in the morning for a honeymoon. He'd come through the war all right — this was in 1946, and everyone was in high spirits. Such festivity there'd been — people drinking their toast, and all the good wishes! Such a lovely wedding; Miss Rosalind was a beautiful bride. And then' — her voice faltered — 'the accident.'

I said nothing, just waited for her to resume.

Obviously the last long statement had tired her. She was breathing more quickly, and I could hear a faint wheezing of her chest. It was a relief to see her fetch a small bottle from her pocket, take out a pill and swallow it.

Then, after a moment, and a little cough, she started off again. 'Two planes collided in mid air, and fell on the Hall. There'd been an air show somewhere that day. Nothing was left but rubble and burning corpses.'

'How — awful.'

'Yes. Most of the house was gone and

170

everyone in it. I only escaped because I'd nipped out to take a bit of the cake to my sister who was an invalid and lived in the village.'

I felt suddenly abashed — distressed by the old lady's reliving of the experience.

'It's upset you,' I said awkwardly. 'I'm sorry.'

For a brief instant the suggestion of a smile touched the wrinkled lips and changed her. I envisaged the aged woman as the girl she'd been herself when attending the child or children of the great house that had once stood there — faithful, kind, and devoted; the loss she must have felt at their sudden cruel destruction. The shock that had impelled her to spend the rest of her life on the terrain where the family had once lived and loved. As if sensing my train of thought, she said, 'I've not spent my life fretting. They wouldn't have wanted it. I was left a tidy little sum — sufficient to buy this plot of land and have this house built. The master was a good man, and I was with them many years. I have my cat. Here he is now — ' She looked towards the door which had opened sufficiently to show the whiskered face of a large, golden-eyed, black cat pushing its furry presence through. 'Meet Mr Thomson,' she said as it entered, bushy tail held aloft, and after a speculative pause came towards me and rubbed its face against my leg. 'I should have known something had happened,' she went on, 'he was all restless the other night, and my electricity failed — '

'Oh?'

She nodded. 'It does, you know, when the past takes over. This house is blotted out for a time. Everything here is darkened but I don't worry. I know that they're still there — all of them and the house. But it was Miss Rosalind's night, and her young husband's. It's true, you know, real love never dies. You can't kill it — whatever happens in the world.'

'I should like to think so,' I said getting up, inwardly comparing her philosophy with the current ways of the space-age world. 'I hope you're right.'

'Perhaps you'll find out,' she remarked, as I went to the door. 'I'm sorry I couldn't have been more help to you, young man. Occasionally I've had others enquiring. Not often though. I'm considered by most to be just a fuddy-duddy of an old woman — isn't that what they call my kind nowadays?' She shook her head, 'Despite their cleverness these scientist folks and what you call philosophers don't get far, for all their 'isms this and 'isms that. And what good are brains without happiness? That's the heart of it all I say. Happiness. I wish you much of it.' She grasped my hand. It felt soft and wrinkled but warm. She was breathing more rapidly again, and I knew I mustn't tire her further. But before I left, she added, 'You're one of the few, I told you, didn't I? Tales have got about, of course. But the Hall was really only ever visible properly from your side of the hill. And there are very few in the world with the eyes to see anyway. That's the sadness of it. I can't explain more. Think yourself privileged to have seen a picture of Miss Rosalind as I knew her — brushing her long, lovely hair.'

A minute later I was walking down the path of her small garden to the narrow lane leading down the moor.

I told myself that the vision I'd had must have been a photograph somehow retained on the ether and reproduced under certain elemental conditions. Further, I would probably never get.

But I had learned something else. What was it she'd said — 'Real love never dies'.

And my wife and I had truly loved once.

I determined to write to her that very day. Quite a different one from the cruel note already started.

We would begin again.

The Nice Child

'Such a nice, well-behaved child.'

'So quiet and unassuming.'

'I always sense a certain sadness in her.'

'That's natural, natural. You can't help feeling sorry for her.'

Such remarks were commonplace when applied to Josie Wayne.

This, of course, was many years ago when quietness and good behaviour were considered virtues.

Josie's appearance reflected her reputation. At nine years of age she was pale complexioned with silky straight hair of a nondescript shade, parted in the middle, and drawn up in hair ribbon above a heart-shaped face possessing widely set blue-grey eyes and a perfectly shaped mouth that could smile on occasion shyly, but with winning charm.

As she lived in the country with her father, and as there was no suitable school nearby, she had a governess at home. She had little chance of meeting other children, and those she *did* contact at village fêtes or on other organized events, found her peculiar and lost their playfulness in her presence, so her social life was limited.

Her father, Godfrey Wayne, was a professor of philosophy at Calebridge College ten miles away on the outskirts of the nearest town. He was a handsome, somewhat remote figure, much sought after by women colleagues and female students, but, since his wife's death, had determinedly refused any serious involvement or commitment to matrimony.

Josie adored him.

Her mother, Godfrey's wife, had died in a mental home when her young daughter was a baby of only six months. The birth had been a difficult one, which apparently had been too much for her. She'd never taken to the child. The shock, it was said, had killed her.

So Josie really had never had what is referred to as a completely normal childhood.

And she knew it.

In a rather *un*childlike way she was clever.

Most other children, she realized very early, had mothers *and* fathers to love them. She had only her father, and sometimes he seemed almost unaware of her existence. As time went by the secret inner necessity that he care for her all the more deeply because of the loss of a mother grew and deepened in her passionately. After all, she argued to herself, you couldn't expect 'Willie' — Miss Willis, her governess — to give love. The child doubted that the plain, middle-aged spinster had any affection in her, although actually she was very fond of her young charge.

From earliest days, Josie, in her quiet sensitive way, had been trying every devious way to win her handsome father's attention. At times she succeeded, but not as successfully as she wished.

It was during this formative period that she discovered Adrian. Adrian became her confidant, and with his help she discovered and developed the strange gift she possessed of 'wishing'.

If she wished it to rain, for instance, it generally soon happened, provided she wished hard enough, and with his help.

Adrian became her close friend.

He was like the knight she'd taken his name from in a fairy book — brave and handsome, almost as handsome as her father. She always closed her eyes tightly when she wanted him for a 'wishing' session, and he would be there — a strong thought-form. So real that she believed one day she'd see him with her eyes open.

So life was tolerable because she was no longer lonely. And her peculiar gift made her feel superior to other children who thought her odd.

She was clever at lessons, but when she was in her tenth year Miss Willis, who had failed to find any response in her to any overtures of affection she made, confided to Godfrey that she was mildly perturbed.

'I'm a little concerned about Josie,' she told him one day when the child was out of hearing.

He looked up sharply from his desk where he was reading notes he'd made for an essay.

'Why? Isn't she working?'

'Oh, yes. She's really very bright, and I'm sure considerably ahead of most children her age, but — ' She broke off slightly embarrassed.

'Well? What is it, Miss Willis? Not her health, I hope?'

'Oh, no. I'm not suggesting anything wrong with her physically. But I *have* wondered if perhaps she wasn't ready for school now. Oh, don't think I want to leave or anything like that — ' Her tone quickened. 'It's just that she hasn't really any friends of her own age, and — '

He was slightly irritated. 'Go on, yes?'

'She talks to herself rather frequently recently,' the governess said, taking the plunge. 'I've heard her more than once, and if she had other children round her, she wouldn't have to.'

He gave a short laugh of relief. 'So *that's* what's worrying you? My dear Miss Willis, if you'd known as many intelligent youngsters as I have you'd know it was quite a habit with some. Acting, you see. She's probably trying to imagine herself a Garbo or Ingrid Bergman. I can assure you there's simply nothing at all sinister or unusual about childish fantasies.'

At fourteen, her demure looks held an elusive almost elfin quality. Her devotion to her father had not decreased with the passing of time, but rather deepened to an obsession of which Adrian was her only confidant. More than ever their 'wishing sessions' concentrated on the professor. If, for instance, she had a sudden desire to go with Miss Willis on a shopping spree for the purpose of purchasing something new to wear that would please him, the opportunity invariably presented itself — *provided* the wish was strong enough.

Then the rain, of course.

There was always the rain.

On one occasion when her father was due to open what Josie considered a stupid open-air bazaar, she spent two hours in the garden willing, with Adrian's help, a wet day ahead.

'He's tired, Adrian,' she whispered urgently — which in fact was true — 'help me.' And her knight was there beside her, gallant in silver armour, golden head turned upwards to the already darkening sky.

For hours it rained. The fête was spoiled.

Generally her wishes were positive and harmless — until the coming of Ginette.

Then the whole tempo of her days changed.

Ginette was a new member to the staff of the college where until then Godfrey had ruled his own sphere in splendid isolation. She in no way threatened his supreme authority, but she certainly diverted his social interests, and life, for him, took on a new dimension. In appearance she was tall, rather large, good-looking in a Swedish way that had an air of Bergman about it.

From the moment they met, Josie hated the newcomer. She was, of course, wise, and gave her polite quiet little girl smile, when her father said in a more robust manner than usual, 'Josie, my dear, this is Miss Leon, a new' — a perceptible pause — 'partner in my department. I'm sure that in the future you two are going to be great friends.'

Not until that first horrible interview was

over did Josie allow the scowl to pucker her forehead. Then, on the first opportunity, she ran into the garden to find Adrian.

'She's *awful*,' she breathed, with clenched fists, heart beating rapidly against her slim body. 'She'll spoil everything. *Everything*. Adrian! — we've got to do something.'

She just shut her eyes and wished and wished and *wished*. The intensity of her concentration sent shuddering sparks of golden light against the velvet blackness of her screwed-up lids, and when she opened them again the quivering vision of Adrian blotted out the patterned background of leaves and trees, leaving only him — her server as ever come to do her will.

The moment was brief, but she knew he understood. The large domineering woman was a threat to her own future with her father.

She sensed it; *knew* it. So did Adrian now.

An opportunity would come to end the dreadful situation, and when it did Adrian would know what to do.

With this knowledge fixed firmly in her thoughts, Josie forced herself to be calm and wait as patiently as possible for the happening.

It wasn't easy.

The mere knowledge of Ginette's existence
— that she must wait for her father's arrival
at the college each day with some new plan
of work or combined interest ahead, made
her feel mildly sick. And, as the days passed,
bringing fresh liveliness to the professor's
eyes, a new bounciness of manner and
spring to his step, the terrible dread of
losing his interest intensified in the young
girl's mind.

Her own birthday brought the crisis.

Every year, she remembered, until then,
the event had been celebrated by a special tea
and cake, while Godfrey took a holiday from
college to spend the afternoon with her.

This year it was different.

The cake — except for an extra candle
— was set ready as usual with special
sandwiches on the table in the lounge,
where french windows opened to a terrace
overlooking the garden in the autumn
sunlight. This year, however, there were
four people instead of three, herself and
Miss Willis, and the overpowering statuesque
Ginette Leon.

To do her justice, Ginette did her very best
to be nice to Josie and had even brought her
a box of coffee-cream chocolates which the
professor had confided to his colleague that
she liked.

184

Josie could hardly resist throwing them in her face.

But she simply said 'thank you' in her polite, demure way with a faint smile on her sweet mouth meant to portray pleasure. Somehow the farce, the pretences of the occasion, were endured.

The climax came when Godfrey announced that he and their guest, after taking a brief 'look in' at the college, were visiting a certain theatre in the town where a cousin of Ginette's was appearing with a repertory company in a series of Shakespearean plays.

Miss Willis had already absented herself, leaving the little trio alone.

Josie was speechless with anger and disappointment. Always before her father had spent the rest of her birthday about the house or garden, or preparing his notes for the week ahead. Through her daze of misery she heard him explain, 'hardly your cup of tea, my dear. A modernized programme. Next year perhaps — '

The rest of his words died in her ears. 'Next year — next year!' What use was *next year* — when this odious Boadicea of a woman — yes, that's what she was, a Boadicea, far more formidable than Bergman, fighting everyone for her own ends — would probably have *married* him, her father, the one being she cared about in all the world except for Adrian.

That was the reason the dreadful Ginette was so absurdly dressed up in blue silk, Josie told herself coldly — when she could think clearly — it hadn't been for her birthday party at all: and anyway blue was the wrong colour for such a large, pompous creature. It was *her* shade, Josie Wayne's. How *dare* she?

For a brief session cold rage replaced all other emotions through which she heard her father saying he was going to make sure there was sufficient petrol in the car. 'So you wait here, my dear,' he told Ginette. 'I'm sure you two can find something to talk about while I see everything's in order.' He gave a stupid smile that made Josie wince, then left the room humming something quite out-of-character for him but all the rage at the time, 'People will say we're in love' from *Oklahoma*.

Ginette turned to the girl. 'You are lucky to have such a lovely home, Josie,' she said with a deliberate attempt to be friendly, 'and such a kind parent.'

'Yes.'

A faint pucker of bewilderment creased the wide brow. 'I hear you're very good at making up little stories,' the tormentor continued, saying quite the wrong thing. 'That's interesting; I'm sure my — your father — will be very proud indeed if his daughter turns out to be a famous novelist one day.'

Stupid creature! Josie thought contemptuously. From that moment any faint remorse she might have felt at the decision forming in her mind, vanished completely.

This was the opportunity she'd been waiting for.

She made a pretence of taking a crumb of cake from the decorated dish, but was seeing only the long, shining paper knife lying by the window with a half-open book on a small pedestal round table.

Everything then became very clear. From a corner of one eye she saw the large figure of Ginette Leon pass, heard her sigh before she went through on to the terrace and stood there, tall, dominant, hands on the rail which Josie knew was weak.

Josie closed her eyes.

'Adrian,' she breathed. 'Adrian — help me.'

Never had she wished so hard before.

There was a crackling sound in her ear — a brief vivid flash of blinding light as the silvered form of Adrian shattered all other details of the room, sweeping the glinting paper knife into a weapon of legendary vengeance that struck sideways across Josie's tensed vision towards the obtrusive female silhouette on the terrace.

Ginette stood there with hands on the weakening terrace rail when it gave, taking her with tumbled masonry and a wild cry to the stone paving above the lawn below. For a second or two, Josie waited until the normal details of the lounge registered, then she turned and walked automatically to her own bedroom nearby. There was a pause before the shouting and pattering of feet started.

When they found her, Josie was still sitting erect on her bed, staring into space.

'Shock!' was the doctor's verdict later. 'The poor child must have witnessed or heard the dreadful incident. It will take time, but she's young. She'll recover.'

There was nothing, of course, to connect her with the tragedy — or the macabre details connected with it. How, for instance, had the sharp paper knife become so deeply embedded in the unfortunate woman's side? She had died of course the moment her head struck the cold paving, so the knife alone could not be blamed, despite the bright blood staining the blue silk. But there were no fingerprints except the professor's and hers on the handle.

He, poor man, was devastated. Everyone at the college had been aware of his growing affection — or rather passion — for the lady, and for some little time he had let it be known that they intended to marry in the future. The only reasonable conclusion therefore — as announced by the coroner later — was that she had been idly playing with the knife, which was valuable and of Oriental origin — and fallen on it as the rail gave. Sympathies were expressed to the bereaved and shocked gentleman who only a week before the incident occurred had made arrangements to replace the failing structure.

'I shall never forgive myself,' he told his daughter many times during the following months. 'I should have had the rail repaired long ago. It is all my fault — ' He broke off miserably, looking drawn and old.

'Oh, no, Papa,' Josie said, putting an arm round him comfortingly. 'And,' she said, looking at him fondly, 'you still have me.'

'Ah, yes. Thank God for my Josie.' His gaze was dimmed with gratitude.

Most people thought the same.

Such a nice child.

The Chair

At first, when Cassandra and Bertrand Sherne moved into their mutual home, everything appeared highly satisfactory. They had been married at the respective mature ages of thirty-eight and forty, and the flat seemed admirably suited to their requirements. It had been converted from the ground floor of a towered late-Victorian house in a select suburb of Bournsea, with a wide garden in front and quiet occupants above. At the side a road lined by pine-trees known as Chalsford Chine, sloped down to sand dunes bordering the sea. It was a 'nice' neighbourhood still adhering strictly to 'class' distinction and tradition, which would be valuable, Bertrand considered, for making helpful personal and business contacts.

He was a conservative type of man, nice-looking in a quiet way, with shrewd eyes and a polite manner, wearing expensive suits of the perennial well-cut brand. His business, following a mediocre start in life as a designer, was antiques; and with a little financial ballast from Cassandra, he'd recently taken up a partnership in an established Bournsea firm. The prospects appeared good, since the partner in question was already over eighty and thinking of retiring. Cassandra too was knowledgeable in such matters, having had access for the last fifteen years to a considerable number of the country's stately homes.

She was a social correspondent on a well known women's magazine, and much of her life was spent in private visits and interviews that were rewarding both financially and from an aesthetic point of view.

So neither of them had time to be bored. A daily woman was engaged for the mornings to keep the place clean and tidy, and to see that no speck of dust or stain marred their floors or furniture, which was mostly antique. She was indeed, as Cassandra often remarked, 'a treasure among treasures'.

From time to time valuable additions were made to the environment; a piece of porcelain perhaps, or bronze; maybe an occasional table from the shop exchanged for one of less value purchased for their home earlier. Bertrand developed a keen eye for spotting a bargain in pictures, and had bought at a country sale a begrimed small oil in a dark frame that when cleaned carefully had proved indisputably to be a Vermeer.

During the first six months of their

marriage both could be considered in their own ways as 'experts', hovering delicately with anticipatory pleasure on the fringe of Bournsea's select set, or 'upper ten' in bygone terminology.

Bournsea itself was a retirement paradise for the rich where wealthy Americans visited their yacht-owning friends, savouring the unshaken and unshakable hierarchy of the English ruling classes which even in the late seventies retained its formidable tradition of owning half the world — if only in its pocket. It was indeed one of the last outposts of the Empire; scarred by merely a handful of modern villas and a small housing estate on the outskirts.

Wide tree-lined avenues and chines bordered its expensive shopping centre, and although tourists of a lesser social brand visited during the summer, they seldom returned to pollute the area. Bournsea had an aura of its own that was discouraging and discomforting to any new breed of humanity; all of which was highly satisfactory to the Shernes.

An appreciation of antiques after all, was the heritage, like blue-blood, of countless generations of breeding; but if on occasion the blue blood of their clientele might be missing, the sad fact could be overlooked providing sufficient money were there.

So an air of complacency settled its comfortable aura about the Shernes at the commencement of their life together.

Because of the secret yearnings of wealthy wives and widows to be interviewed and photographed for women's magazines, Cassandra gradually found herself accepting dinner dates with the elite, accompanied frequently by Bertrand, who inwardly squirmed with pleasure when the host of the household addressed him as 'old boy', the prelude to asking his opinion concerning a rare piece of furniture or Ming.

On these occasions, Bertrand had sometimes to be more ambiguous than he would have liked, but clever enough to disguise a certain lack of knowledge under a veneer of weighty consideration.

'You're really a subtle old thing, darling,' Cassandra said once after just such an occasion. 'Old Monkley set a real poser for you, didn't he? I could have screamed with delight at the way you handled him. And that wife of his . . . what a fool. *Really*. Still, you mark my words, this evening will pay off; I'm not even so sure she didn't have a sneaking yen for you. Cultivate it, darling, it'll pay dividends.'

Bertrand frowned.

'At times, Cassandra, I fancy a coarse touch in you.'

She shrugged her shoulders, glancing over one with a touch of coquetry that mildly stimulated yet irritated him.

'And at times I'm quite sure, Bertrand, you're more than a bit of a prude.'

She had a splendid back . . . taut buttocks, erect spine, with rather large firmly rounded shoulders over which the thick dark hair fell in lustrous waves.

At that particular moment she was standing by the mirror undressing for bed. Her satin slip had fallen to the floor at her feet, and she was obviously relishing a dose of lovemaking.

But Bertrand, who had a hard streak in him, and knew quite well what she was up to, pretended to be obtuse, and merely replied with a hint of contempt, 'Get something on, for Heaven's sake. You look . . . '

'Yes?' Her voice had sharpened.

'Well, not exactly one's vision of tempting virginity,' he told her shortly. 'What I mean is, sexy by-play doesn't suit you. Hang it all, Cass, you're no Twiggy. And in case you didn't know it, you're putting on weight. You should watch it.'

She flushed. 'How crude. And how . . . *bourgeois*,' spitting the word out with

197

wild-cat intensity. All the same she slung a wrap round her shoulders, thinking maybe it was true, about the weight business. It would be too awful if just at this most promising highlight of her career she was to develop the spreading curves of the wealthy stout matrons she so effectively flattered between the pages of the glossy magazines. She must endeavour to control her appetite a little and concentrate on vitamins.

Bertrand's words had hurt; and there was no lovemaking that night. But when the first shock and sting had departed she realized that this was not the first time during the past week he'd thrown out a subtle snub. The niggling problem was, why? There was no other woman, she was certain of this. Bertrand's libido was of a particularly fastidious brand, as were his code of ethics and social behaviour. Besides she was generally available for the brief interludes when sexual need temporarily obscured his first enduring passion for antiques.

True, their lovemaking had always been of the somewhat clinical and orderly genre. But she was a woman after all, and it was grossly unfair of him, she decided, to wish to taunt her . . . especially as she was so careful always to camouflage the fact that it was through *her* career, and her own very satisfying bank balance, that Bertrand had been enabled to follow his chosen bent.

Perhaps she had been over-generous. It could be. Sometimes an occasional home truth at an opportune moment was necessary in order to conserve the status quo.

After reaching this decision Cassandra was careful to apply it. Not often, but increasingly as the days passed. The trouble was that Bertrand, instead of reacting according to plan, appeared increasingly more indifferent to Cassandra's mature charms, with the result that her planned barbed comments became eventually habitual.

When autumn came, with Nature turning from its most prolific season to an abundancy of rich content and colourful verdure of falling leaf and yellowing moorlands, she did her best to heal the insidiously encroaching rift between them, and suggested they should take a holiday; abroad perhaps, the South of France or Majorca, or if her husband preferred, one of the smaller of the Channel Isles.

Bertrand was not interested. 'I can't understand you,' he said. 'October's one of our best months for business. It would be ridiculous to take off now.'

'Why?' Cassandra queried sharply. 'November and December mean Christmas sales. You're becoming a bit of a fuddy-duddy you know. Except for the house party weekends which mean hard work for me, and your own mooching around with auctioneers, we go nowhere. Nowhere.' Her voice had risen. She was breathing quickly.

'Why should we?' Bertrand remarked calmly. 'We're all right here, aren't we?'

'All right? After only a year of marriage? Do you really expect me to relish every spare evening we have together sitting in front of puerile television programmes before making for the marital bed . . . which let me tell you has been decidedly chilly lately? You talk of my figure; but what of yours?'

'Mine?' Bertrand interrupted before she could finish. 'I don't think you can accuse *me* of being overweight, Cassie; in fact I think I wear extremely well.'

'Yes,' she agreed, but with a dark undertone in her voice. 'Like a piece of furniture. Like that damned chair you're so fond of. You watch out, my dear, or you'll find yourself glued to it one day. As a matter of fact it was a mistake getting it. It's far too large, and the rush seat's wearing. I got a nasty jab on my leg the other day. From a nail or something . . . '

'That chair was made by a craftsman. It has no nails.'

'Whatever it was . . . straw, nail, wood, I don't care. It *hurt*. I had to put disinfectant on the scratch. And it's cumbersome to move. Mrs Weeks told me she couldn't manage it without bruising herself . . . so I have to get on my knees and dust all round and underneath myself.'

Bertrand smiled with a hint of malice. 'You have well-padded knees, my love. I'm sure they'll survive. Besides, you, of all people, should appreciate its artistic worth.'

'I thought it was a bargain at the beginning,' Cassandra conceded. 'But now, I'm not so sure. It has splinters.'

'*Splinters?* You must be mad. The woodwork's solid polished teak. Smooth as glass. Has been for centuries.'

'Glass can cut,' she said shortly.

'Well, if you can show me one single rough patch in that chair's frame,' Bertrand told her, 'I'll eat my hat; and more. I'll . . . I'll do what you suggest, get rid of it.'

'Come along then,' she said.

'Now?'

'Yes.'

'I'm feeling peckish. We'll have a bite first.'

'No we won't. I'm sorry . . . I want it settled. It's important. The casserole can wait.'

Seeing her mind was made up he shrugged impatiently, clicked his teeth, and followed her grudgingly from the kitchen to the sitting room. The rush-seated chair stood in a corner conveniently placed between a window and the fireplace, at the right distance for viewing television. The high back, which was carved, sloped at an angle to take cushions comfortably. The arms too were carved; the legs no more than a foot in height, claw-footed, splayed outwards.

In its way it was a curiosity, and hard to place as belonging to any exact period. Bertrand had suggested early Georgian, but Cassandra had thought Victorian. When Bertrand had brought it back from the auctioneer's following a sale, she hadn't cared for it, though admitting it had a certain uniqueness.

'*Unique?*' he'd said then, 'it's more than that, it's a treasure. What's more, the design's just right for my back.'

Bertrand's back which had been weak as a child, was his unfailing excuse for obtaining or retaining any domestic 'piece' or appliance that took his fancy. So Cassandra had known that in their home it would stay.

Which it had.

Until now.

But she was damned if she'd keep the

cumbersome thing any longer. When she moved it she got great bruises on her thighs. Twice she'd been jabbed by something from under the seating, and once when she'd turned it to reach a reel of cotton that had rolled underneath, a hefty clawed foot had somehow hit her own and stubbed her big toe. The bruise had lasted a fortnight. For Bertrand to say the chair was a craftsman's work was ridiculous. There were splinters under the arms, and even the rush-work was imperfect, as scratches on her wrists and calves showed.

'Well,' she heard Bertrand saying, 'where is it? What do you want to show me? What's wrong with it?'

'Put your hand under the seat,' she said, feeling coolly triumphant, 'and the arms too. Go on, *examine* it. You'll see.'

Bertrand bent down and, holding it with one hand, let the other travel the whole width and extent of the rush base and wooden frame. After a minute's probing he looked up at her, shaking his head; then lifting the chair sideways he examined the arms and legs thoroughly. 'It hasn't a scratch anywhere,' he stated, straightening up abruptly. 'The chair's in perfect condition. As for splinters . . . you certainly didn't get them here. More likely from that bookcase thing you would insist on having, though I told you it wasn't genuine.'

She stared.

'I don't believe it. It was when I touched the *arms*. I tell you, Bertrand, it's a . . . a devil.'

He laughed derisively.

'If you want proof, *feel* it. Examine it yourself.' He paused, adding with a touch of malice, 'Or are you afraid? Is that it? Believe in hoodoos, do you?'

Cassandra almost said, Yes, I do . . . in this case. It's malignant . . . a horrible thing.

But she had the sense not to; and after a moment forced herself to run a hand over the woodwork and frame, and under the rush seat. What Bertrand said was quite true, or appeared to be. There were no splinters or rough places, and certainly no hard pieces of rush or wire that could have inflicted the jab on her leg.

'I don't understand,' she said slowly, reflectively. 'Unless . . . have *you* been at work on it, Bertrand?'

He laughed. 'What time have I had? And why on earth wouldn't I have told you if it was like that? Do pull yourself together, Cass, and use your common sense. You weren't keen on the chair from the start, and consequently blame it for any scratch or bruise you get about the house. It's as simple as that.'

But of course it wasn't.

As the days passed her suspicions concerning the chair intensified. Occasionally that autumn, when she returned to the flat earlier than Bertrand, she fancied that although she was careful not to touch it, its mere presence as a dark shape in the evening light emitted an evil aura which was almost a sneer. A sneer of triumph. Once she even had the impression of a shadowy form hunched against the woodwork. She rubbed her eyes, looked again, and it was gone. Telling herself it was all imagination and that her nerves were wrong, she turned abruptly and went to the kitchen, busying herself with the evening meal; but she was careful not to enter the sitting room until her husband came back.

Bertrand had had a particularly good day at the shop, and was so occupied with self-satisfaction he quite failed to notice the pallor and set strain of his wife's face. It was as though, she thought bitterly, he didn't really see her clearly any more. All that mattered to him was his business, his bargains, and his precious chair.

The chair.

She puzzled her mind continually how to get rid of it without evoking too much resentment from Bertrand, but with no success. Bertrand, in his way, was dedicated and stubborn; and although superficially controlled and quiet-mannered, possessed a dark temper beneath the veneer. If she sent it to another saleroom he'd find out where and bring it back again. If she bribed the dustmen to take it, he'd somehow get the truth out of her and the same day the odious thing would be in its corner once more, more firmly established than ever.

There was an axe of course, in the cellar. She could . . . but at that point her thoughts boggled. No *no*. Never that. The effect on their marriage of hacking the thing to pieces was just too terrible to contemplate. As the days passed, concentration on her own work faltered. Her contributions to the magazine began to lose zest and colour. Invitations to fashionable dinner-parties began to abate, and one day she was called to London to the editor's office and asked politely but meaningfully if anything was worrying her, as certain articles appeared to be less interesting than formerly.

'Perhaps you need a holiday,' the suave voice continued, when Cassandra replied in the negative. 'Why don't you take a week off, or a fortnight perhaps? Wouldn't it be possible for you and your husband to have a change somewhere together? It's wonderful what even a brief respite from routine can do for restoring enthusiasm in one's work.'

There was a pause before Cassandra replied, 'I really don't think that's necessary. If my columns have been unsatisfactory lately, I'm sorry. It won't happen again. I've had private worries that have preyed on my mind. I realize now I shouldn't have let them. Not to the extent they have.'

'Well . . . ' The blue eyes behind the desk which could appear so coldly remote yet discouraging at the same moment glanced away for a second, as the calm voice continued, 'It's up to you, naturally. But remember personnel is always available to give help and advice to our staff when required. Your work has been much appreciated in the past; it would be a great pity for standards to drop . . . not only on *your* account, but the magazine's. We have to see that our reputation is kept always up to scratch. I'm sure you understand, Mrs Sherne?'

'Perfectly,' Cassandra replied firmly. 'I can assure you you'll have no further need to complain.'

And in the weeks following she saw this was so, devoting herself with fanatical zeal to her columns, tensing herself to meet the challenge of interviews and social commitments with an intense interest and façade of bright repartee and flattering comments that quickly established her again as a firm favourite with readers.

She was seldom at home that winter, which kept her mind from morbid reflections concerning the chair.

But Bertrand started to complain.

'We may both have careers,' he pointed out, 'but I assume we're also married. The point is, who to? The work or the individual?'

Cassandra laughed jarringly. 'Oh Bertrand . . . *really*! Sarcasm doesn't suit you. Besides, at *our* age . . . '

'Age?' he echoed shortly. 'If I remember correctly it was you who used to go for the lovey-dovey stuff. Quite the coquette you were at the beginning, swinging your hips, flashing your eyes . . . ' His lips suddenly tightened, his jaw thrust out in a most un-Bertrand like way, before he continued, 'What is it, Cassie? Got someone else tucked away, have you? A little hidey-hole where you can be together while I spend my evenings alone eating a ham sandwich for my meal or something from the fridge?'

His eyes, as his hands closed on her shoulders, held a hard cold gleam that almost frightened her.

She shook herself free.

'Don't be a fool,' she snapped, 'you know better than that. I'm not the kind for any hole-and-corner business. If I wanted a lover you'd know all about it. So for heaven's sake, Bertrand . . . ' She broke off, turned away, swamped by a sudden sense of dejection. He followed her to the door, muttering, with a hint of shame in his voice, 'Sorry, I didn't mean . . . I don't know what's got into me . . . into both of us lately . . . snapping and arguing. Overwork maybe.'

But she knew it wasn't overwork; it was the chair. That damned, dark, evil chair.

That same night, when Bertrand was sleeping in the large double bed they shared, she was startled by a furtive movement below. Thinking she might have left a window unlatched, or some prowler was about with the possibility in mind of making a break-in, she got up, slipped on a wrap, and without disturbing Bertrand who objected to being woken suddenly, she went downstairs softly, torch in hand to investigate. At the foot of the stairs she noticed with relief that a wind had risen driving a spatter of rain against the front door and under it. The rug in the hall was rising and flapping gently from the gust of air. We really must get some draught-proof rubber fixed to the woodwork, Cassandra decided, as she bent down to roll the rug up. It was something they'd been meaning to put right since moving in; but with so much else to attend to, it had been pushed aside until a more opportune moment.

Ugh! but how cold it was. And eerie, with the darkness outside caught into a streaking slashing shadow from the rain.

She drew her wrap close at the neck, and was passing the sitting-room towards the stairs when something took her attention.

Her blood froze.

The door was half open, giving an unobstructed view of Bertrand's cherished chair in the corner. And then it started . . . the tapping furtive sound she'd heard from upstairs. She stood motionless, horrified, as the torch automatically swung its fitful beam full on the scene, bringing the skeleton-like contours of bony hands into focus . . . ugly, gnarled hands clutching both wooden arms. Then, very gradually, the toe of a boot projected, moving with horrible precision, up and down, up and down; a dark shape against the dark shadows, emitting a click like a hammer's tap as the heel struck the floor. Unable to tear her eyes away, Cassandra watched the fitful light curdle into the thrust-forward furred shape of a man's form with a disc of yellowish white above it . . . a face; but a face that was almost featureless except for the holed shadows of eyes and sunken jaws. The head's motion was as regular as each beat of the large foot, and equally malignant. Only once did it turn purposefully, staring her straight in the face. The gap of the mouth darkened into a grin so malevolent everything suddenly went from her, taking her into a thickening void of tumbling shapes and terror.

Then she screamed.

Bertrand found her minutes later in the hall, hunched against the wall. She was conscious, but not yet fully recovered from the faint.

'What on earth's the matter?' Bertrand said sharply, helping her to her feet. 'Are you sick?'

She shook her head. In the flood of the hall light she looked ghastly, pale-lipped and still shaking.

'Then what is it? Why are you wandering about at such a godforsaken hour?' His grip tightened on her arm. 'Cass . . .' he urged with more sympathy, realizing she'd really had a shock of some kind.

'Come on now . . . ' urging her towards the sitting room. 'A drink first, then tell me all about it.'

But with surprising strength she pulled herself away.

'No, not there. Not in *there* . . . '

'But . . . '

Bertrand stared at her uncomprehendingly, then switched on the sitting-room light, searching briefly for any sign of intrusion or indication of disorder.

There was none. Everything was in place and perfect order, chairs, table, and chest with his gold cigarette case lying there just as he'd left it hours before. If there'd been a thief about, the case, surely, would have been the first item to attract attention.

'You must have had a nightmare,' he said, before turning again to his wife. But she'd gone, and was already halfway up the stairs, rushing, stumbling, then pulling herself on again with unnerving desperation.

'Cass . . . ' He hurried after her, and did his best to calm her down. Later, when she'd had a sedative and hot drink she became coherent, but completely indifferent to his assurances that there was no one else in the flat, and that the intruder she *thought* she'd seen in the sitting-room had been merely imagination.

'Maybe you should have a change?' he said moodily at last, when she still refused to be convinced. 'We can't go on like this. You . . . '

'Why can't you get rid of that chair?' she said coldly, with a dull strained look in her eyes. 'Whatever you say, it's . . . it's a bad thing. *You* may not believe in influences, or ghosts, or witchcraft, neither did I before this happened. But I've changed my mind now. I *know*, Bertrand.'

'What do you mean *know*?'

'Just that. There are things here that can't be explained — rationally. Beastly things. And all concerned with that wretched chair. Oh Bertrand . . . ' Her voice softened, became pleading, her whole personality emitting an innate femininity that should have aroused his compassion.

But all he felt, though he did his best to hide it, was a mixture of irritation and contempt. This was not the Cassandra he'd married, the tower of strength and female dignity to give balance and assurance to his life; this was a sick hysterical creature appearing to him rather ridiculous in her maturity.

'I'll think about it,' he told her, knowing very well he had no intention of doing so. 'The important thing now is to get some

213

sleep. In the morning you'll probably laugh at yourself.'

But in the morning everything was the same, although Cassandra, physically recovered from the shock put on a charade of aloofness, refusing to discuss the matter.

When Bertrand referred to it tentatively, she said curtly, 'Forget it. I'll see your night's rest is not disturbed again, Bertrand.'

'It wasn't just that,' he remarked uncomfortably, 'I was worried.'

'Were you indeed? How kind of you.'

'And there's no need to get into a huff about it. Any man would be, to find his wife in such a state at midnight. From your scream I thought at least you'd been attacked . . . '

'Well, as you see, I hadn't. I'm perfectly sound in wind and limb, and mind,' she replied, 'with my virginity . . . or *near*-virginity unsullied.'

He pretended to ignore the crack, but after that matters became cooler between them. Bertrand obviously had no intention of getting rid of the chair. It was, he said, the most comfortable he'd ever had, and could have been designed for 'viewing'. The word 'viewing' began eventually so to jar Cassandra's nerves she had an impulse to throw a book at his head as he sat complacently in the odious carved piece, hands on the wooden arms, or with one elbow resting at a convenient angle for filling his pipe when necessity demanded. This was another strange thing . . . the pipe. Until the evening of his wife's macabre experience he had never smoked at all, saying tobacco permeated drapes, rugs, and any valuable furnishings they possessed. Now he was becoming a real addict, although at the shop and in salerooms he'd no wish to indulge himself at all, but remained the impeccable distinguished and discriminating Bertrand Sherne so respected by auctioneers and clients alike.

Cassandra managed somehow to retain her job, but the effort took increasing toll of her nervous energy, and she was frequently short-tempered with Bertrand, knowing she was becoming a 'nagger' but unable to control the habit. He curbed a desire to taunt and sting, though at times he had an almost overwhelming impulse to strike her. She was so damned cold and reserved, and . . . and *large*. That was it . . . a large sexy woman with no sex for him any more. A woman he was sick of and no longer wanted, but whom he was possessively determined no other man should have.

Moreover, he couldn't entirely forget her

garbled words on the night in the hall about a male figure in the chair. Maybe it had been an illusion; he was sure it had. But illusions could spring from an unsatisfied need, as any intelligent person knew, and the thought of Cassandra lusting after anyone else infuriated him.

Christmas passed with the minimum of festivities and January was a bleak one for that part of the country, bringing grey seas under sullen skies, filled with periods of rain lashing the town and suburbs into wet uniformity.

Cassandra, inwardly tense and edgy, took herself off on every available opportunity to functions and interviews which she wrote up with a forced highly coloured vitality meant to destroy any lingering doubts concerning her capability. Afterwards, at the wheel of her car once more, driving along wet roads back to Bournsea, a feeling of fatigue and desolation encompassed her. Although she longed to be at home in bed, the thought of reaching the house depressed her. She'd taken to entering by the back door so she didn't have to pass the lounge when she got to the hall. But eventually of course, it was impossible to avoid the room. More often than not she'd find Bertrand seated in the hated chair when she went in, one hand on an arm, the other enclosing the stem of his pipe; a figure that daily, in such a posture, seemed to grow thinner and older, more menacing and similar to the shadowy shape envisaged on that terrifying autumn night. Bertrand's face, too, appeared more sinister and elongated; the eyes narrowed in their sockets, holding a shifty sidelong glance.

She told herself repeatedly she was over-tired, was imagining things, and thought of consulting a doctor or psychologist. Her hand was actually on the point of dialling for an appointment one day, then suddenly she slammed the receiver down.

What was the use? What conclusion could possibly be drawn from the garbled statement of a woman who admitted she was terrified by a chair, except the inevitable explanation of 'neurosis', ('a hallucination, no more, my dear'), with the advice probably of taking a cure in some select rest home, or 'looney bin' as Cassandra termed it, where everything could be sorted out.

Sorted out? The idea was ridiculous. She knew what she knew, and saw and heard. The sitting-room could mostly be avoided except on evenings when Bertrand demanded her presence. But at night as she lay sleepless in bed, nothing could dull the tap-tapping from below; the ghastly rhythmic click as of a heel on the floor or a hammer's knock.

She began to talk in her sleep. Once she woke up suddenly to see in the glow of the bedside lamp Bertrand's face glaring down on her. His eyes were hard and cold, mouth set in a thin cruel line.

'Don't . . . don't . . . ' she was shrieking. 'Oh Isaac, don't . . . '

Bertrand's face came down to hers, almost unrecognizable in its fury. He jerked her fully awake, pulling the nightdress tight at her neck. 'What's that?' he demanded. 'Who's Isaac? You tell me that . . . just tell me, or I'll beat the hell out of you, do you hear? It's what you deserve . . . a sound thrashing.' He was breathing heavily. She couldn't believe this was the man she'd married, the quiet, intellectual Bertrand Sherne.

She pulled herself away and jumped out of bed, clutching her clothes to her, watching him rigidly as he approached, head thrust forward, swaying slightly, a look of such hatred on his face until faintness rose in her with a feeling of nausea and shame. Then suddenly, the rage seemed to evaporate. He straightened up, staring at her blankly.

'What's the matter, Cass?' he asked in a dull voice. 'What are you looking like that for? And why are you standing there?'

'You know,' she said. 'You must know. I had a nightmare, and you attacked me.'

He laughed disbelievingly. 'Another delusion; is that it? Why would I attack you? Good heavens, if you go on this way you'll have us both round the bend. If I have any more of the stupid business you'll have to see a specialist. I'll get him round myself.'

'No you won't,' she flashed back at him. 'If you do I'll tell him the whole truth.'

'About what?' he asked, mildly sarcastic. 'Your chilly behaviour to me and tawdry little affairs with other men behind my back? Your continual erratic night jaunts and stupid delusions?'

'No. You're lying, Bertrand, and you know it. The chair . . . it's the chair.'

'Ha!' he jeered. 'A chair. What do you think any good doctor would make of that, eh? Just think, my dear,' — mockingly — 'well of course . . . Hmm! Women of your age, Mrs Sherne, are inclined to suffer . . . um . . . aberrations at certain times. Perhaps . . . '

'Stop it,' Cassandra said. 'There's nothing wrong with my mind. And just now, though you're unaware of it . . . or pretend to be . . . you are the one needing medical attention. You were quite violent. It's the truth: I swear it.'

Whether he believed her or not she couldn't tell; but after a gradual cessation of argument an uneasy silence developed between them, and presently both a little shamefaced, they went back to bed.

After that, matters though superficially calmer, became really worse. Cassandra, inwardly terrified that she might perhaps be going out of her mind, forced herself to spend certain evenings with Bertrand pretending to watch television although the picture seldom registered. When she glanced towards her husband furtively . . . at his long legs spread out before him, spine slumped against the cushioned chair-back, head tilted, eyes half closed, mouth drawn into a narrowed half-smile of self-satisfaction, it was all she could do to prevent herself saying, 'Stop it, Bertrand. Don't look like that. Stop it . . . stop it.'

Once during the break in the programme he turned his head slowly and asked, 'What's the matter, Cassandra? Why are you staring?'

'I wasn't,' she answered. 'At least . . . you were so still. You haven't spoken for ages. I thought perhaps . . . '

'I was dead?' His voice was light, holding a cruel amusement in it. His whole manner seemed cruel, sadistic, as though he meant to taunt her.

'Dead? What a stupid thing to say.'

'Is it?' He was by then staring reflectively at the ceiling. 'Oh I don't know. We all have to die sometime. Do you ever think of that, Cass? You, me . . . everyone.'

'No. I don't . . . not unless something reminds me,' she said shortly.

'Oh well, that's natural,' he agreed imperturbably, tapping his heel on the floor. 'But there are so many reminders in our business aren't there? Old paintings, old relics, old books . . . yes, books are the most revealing of all I think! I was perusing a volume the other day concerning criminology. It's amazing how many unsolved murders there were in the past. And yet regarding things objectively after a passage of time, it's quite obvious many of the guilty get off scot free, leaving the innocent to pay the price.'

Cassandra shivered.

'Need you talk about such morbid things?'

'Of course not, if it worries you. You're really rather a frightened, emotional sort of creature though, aren't you, Cass? So different from what I imagined when we first met.'

'So are you,' she retorted.

'Ah well, we mustn't bicker. Such a waste of time.' He paused before adding, 'The programme's on again. Let's relax, shall we?'

Relax, relax! she thought initially, how could anyone relax with Bertrand sitting so smugly in that horrible chair tap-tap-tapping with his foot just as though some ancient ritual was driving him? Or something else perhaps . . . something connected with the malignant shadow she'd seen, or thought she'd seen on that ghastly night when her husband had behaved so viciously.

She got up abruptly saying, 'I'm going to bed, I've got a headache.'

'A good idea,' Bertrand agreed. 'I told you you should see a doctor.'

But doctors were no use as Cassandra discovered during the following weeks.

She consulted two, including a nerve specialist. Both informed her she was physically sound, the latter advising her, as she'd quite expected, to take a period of rest at his clinic.

'Nightmares are frequently the result of over-strain or due to some repressed guilt complex,' she was told. 'Possibly sexual problems. Forgive the question . . . but have you a normal marriage, Mrs Sherne?'

'Perfectly,' Cassandra agreed quickly, realizing the appointment had been a complete waste of time. No specialist after all, could be of the simplest help unless she'd confided the true source of the trouble . . . the chair. And this she was determined not to do.

So refusing the suggestion of the clinic and with a pretence of feeling better for the 'little chat' she paid an enormous bill, and returned disheartened, to life in the flat with Bertrand.

Matters gradually worsened.

The first frail days of spring arrived, washed alternatively by thin, windswept rain, and pale sunlight spattering the moors and lanes with gold. It should have been a pleasant period . . . a time of promise and thoughts of summer ahead. But Cassandra, beneath her brittle sophisticated veneer, felt only increasing desolation, which when evening came, sending long fingered shadows across the landscape, was frequently charged with acute terror. Only a fanatical dedication to work saved her from betraying herself. With her hands taut on the steering wheel of her car she drove wildly and far more quickly than she should from home to her various interviews. Occasionally she stopped by a field or in a country lane to light a cigarette and relax into some kind of normality. But always as she neared the flat on her return journey a pall of unease and fear swamped her. And generally, when she went through the hall . . . he would be there. Bertrand's figure seated in the tall-backed chair watching television, with his heel tap-tapping on the floor, a curdle of tobacco smoke spiralling towards the ceiling. And if he wasn't, if he was late from the shop, she'd be aware of something . . . someone in his place; a half glimpsed shadow turned towards her. She'd rush then, up the stairs to her room, where she'd stand for a few moments staring into the mirror, revolted by her own greenish pallor, staring dark eyes and half-open gasping mouth.

Generally after this she'd take a strong brandy and wait seated on the bed, until her nerves and heart steadied. But of course Bertrand noticed. Once when he found her, drink in hand, viewing herself through the glass, he said coldly, 'Aren't you taking too much of that stuff? God! The whole place reeks.' Her reply was garbled and tipsily ridiculous. He began to detest her whining voice in such moods . . . the high flush on her large face which had once been so good-looking. In fact, day by day, dislike grew in him. He wondered how he could ever have found her the slightest bit desirable, least of all have married her. When she wasn't in a mood, complaining or nagging, she seemed forever on his track, following him around the house, trying to tempt him from television with the promise of, 'I've got a surprise in the kitchen, darling . . . one of your favourite tit-bits . . . the one we used to call 'Bertrand's delight'? 'Member?'

He didn't want to remember although he knew she meant some mushroom and tomato concoction that had pleased his palate in their early days. Now, nothing about Cassandra pleased him at all. Neither her cooking, her presence, or her looks. Although she still contrived to look smart when she went on a 'date' she overdid the make-up and it appeared to him that she took a delight in flaunting her figure which had always been sturdy . . . especially the thrusting breasts that nowadays he found positively repugnant. All the same the idea she could be cuckolding him still filled him with increasing hatred, and he found himself frequently wishing something would happen to end their relationship . . . some chance event that would release him from the commitment of marriage . . . some 'act of God' as they put it. The first time he realized the trend of his own wishful thinking he caught himself up abruptly and guiltily dismissed it. But the next occasion was more difficult. And anyway, he told himself, there could be no harm in 'wishing'. Cass was as strong as a bull. She'd go on forever.

As it happened, he was wrong about the 'wishing' business and it was about this time that he became first aware of his own latent powers.

They'd had a row one Sunday afternoon ... started as usual over the chair, and Cassandra had flounced out to the car. A minute later he'd heard the engine start, followed by its acceleration as she turned into the road.

'That's right,' he found himself muttering under his breath, 'go on, go on, smash the car and kill yourself . . . go on, Cass . . . '

She didn't kill herself, but the car was smashed all right, through taking a turn on the wrong side of the road and bumping into a tree.

Following the accident there was a case, naturally, which ended with an endorsement of Cassandra's licence and a hefty fine. All she suffered physically, was a sprained wrist and bruised eye.

Bertrand was infuriated, not only because she had got off so lightly, but because it was *his* car she'd smashed; her own car was at the garage undergoing minor repairs. Still, the fact remained that he'd 'wished' something, and something had happened. Not in the way he'd meant; but the incident started a whole new train of ideas that he instantly proceeded to try out.

Quite small things at first; that Cassandra should lose her purse or cut herself; stub her toe against the dresser, or develop a cold for no reason at all. All manner of unimportant happenings calculated, however, to prove his point.

In the beginning only one suggestion might work; but with practice and more concentration, his successes began to prove more numerous than his failures. He even willed one evening that his wife should take a wrong turning coming back from an interview. And to his immense satisfaction this was exactly what happened. Triumph in his own powers consumed him; became almost a dedication to his inner self. He felt elated, free; confident that at any moment he wished, given the strength of concentration, he could have Cassandra exactly how and where he wanted.

What the ultimate aim was he was not yet fully aware; but day by day, night by night, a dark knowledge gathered in him; subtle yet firm and strong. As strong as the sturdy chair which had become, in a deep primitive way, the symbol of his manhood.

As summer passed to autumn, bringing yellowing skies and early evenings when the light quickly faded hanging its brooding mists over the town and surrounding landscape, Bertrand's evenings seated before the television in the carved oak chair became then obsessional. He would pause there morose and silent, even in Cassandra's presence. Sometimes when she spoke, insisting on his attention, he would turn his head slowly, stare at her briefly from half-closed lids and his face would frighten her, because it was an alien face . . . contemptuous, cold and queerly intimidating. He seldom answered, and she'd leave the room hurriedly, wondering which of them was mad . . . Bertrand or herself.

Upstairs in her room she'd 'take stock of herself' through the mirror, and her own reflection repulsed herself. The large-boned face, with fear-ridden eyes and lines of strain creasing forehead and from nose to jaws, no longer held any pretension to beauty. Once she had at least been comely. Now she felt herself to be a hag. But in the daytime, at least, with the aid of make-up and a series of smart wigs and large tinted glasses that had become the vogue, she somehow contrived to appear a 'personality' and retained her job on the magazine, however tenuously. It was in the evenings that the real nightmare started . . . the evenings when Bertrand had not returned and she had to pass the sitting

228

room. Generally the door was half open
. . . sufficiently so for her to glimpse from the
corner of her eye the shadowy form seated
malignantly in the high-backed chair, one
foot tap-tap-tapping on the floor, yellowish
face half turned towards her. In earlier days,
when the delusion . . . or whatever it was
. . . had first taken root in her mind, she'd
forced herself on, keeping her eyes rigidly
ahead. But eventually the effort had failed.
Some power stronger than her own will
urged her gaze compulsively towards the
hidden horror of the lounge. The horror
of the chair.

One afternoon when she'd returned earlier
than usual to the flat, she knew she couldn't
bear it anymore and in a fit of desperation
rushed to the cellar and snatched the axe
from the corner. She was breathing heavily
when she reached the lounge. Her heart was
pumping painfully against her ribs, her arms
trembling as she raised it high above her
head, bringing it down on the woodwork.
There was a sharp snap and crack; a sense of
writhing as though living matter squirmed.

Then silence for a moment while the mist
cleared from her eyes. She drew a hand
helplessly across her damp forehead. Sweat
streamed in rivulets of fear and despair down
her body. She was suddenly terrified of what

she'd done. But when her sight properly registered she saw to her amazement nothing had happened; nothing but a very faint dent on the teak, and this was quickly fading. She collapsed on to the sofa with her head in her hands, the axe fallen to the floor. Presently she got to her feet, picked up the implement, and went to the door. She glanced back once, and already fancied the shadowy occupant was back again, grimacing from the chair, with such calculated evil she knew any power there was stronger than her own.

Only one course was left to her: she must leave Bertrand, the travesty of their life together; the area, the flat and all it contained . . . most of all the chair.

Once she'd made the decision things seemed less hopeless. She started planning. Obviously there would be no point in informing her husband. He would merely start arguing and perhaps develop one of those queer unpredictable rages that hit him from time to time when she raised any topic concerning his chair. She decided to take off one certain night when she knew he'd be late home, and there'd be no chance of his popping in unexpectedly in business hours or during sales. An evening train to London would put sufficient distance between them for safety. Once there her confidence would be reimbued again; sufficiently so for her to confront him firmly if he arrived at the magazine offices the next day querying her whereabouts and demanding an interview.

She had no intention of leaving a note, or any explanation whatever. He didn't deserve one. And probably, she thought cynically, he wouldn't care so long as the chair remained. The refrain of an old song beat through her brain, 'Me and my Shadow', making her chuckle ironically as she pictured Bertrand night after night seated on the odious thing tap-tap-tapping with his heel on the floor, eyes half closed, waiting for . . . what?

Swiftly she pushed the image behind her, and turned her mind to the more practical details of where she'd stay when she reached town and what personal possessions she'd take. When everything was more or less decided, her depression gave place to a false keyed-up buoyancy that Bertrand found slightly disconcerting. She seldom entered the sittingroom by then, and whenever she passed the door, the air vibrated with her humming, or tumtiddly . . . tum-tum . . . of some old dance hit or new pop item that irritated him profoundly. Had she seen the darkening of his eyes or thin angry curve of his down-turned mouth, the old alarm would have risen in her, sending her scuttling up

231

the stairs. But she was learning gradually to withstand the temptation to throw even a furtive sidelong glance in his direction.

So the days passed. And at last the evening of her flight arrived.

Bertrand, as she'd known, was making his monthly visit to an acquaintance of his, a Colonel Whitworth and his lady, who had a handsome residence in the country fifteen miles away. Both were interested in antiques and 'dear old Georgie' as Bertrand familiarly referred to him, had put him on to many a good thing. He wouldn't have missed one of these assignations for the world. Besides their mutual capacity for scenting a bargain, the colonel was a connoisseur both of food, wines and most good things of this world.

So shortly after her husband had set off, and his car swung out of the gates, Cassandra started packing and realized only at the last minute that she'd forgotten to include one cherished item ... a small porcelain figurine of a china shepherdess which had been her grandmother's. Not only was it of considerable value financially, but sentimentally. She must have it.

The trouble was it had the place of honour on a 'William and Mary' chest in the lounge.

Just for a moment she paused, sickened

at the thought of having to enter that room again. Then bracing herself with the knowledge it would only take a second or two, she rushed downstairs, along the hall, and went in.

At the same moment, though she didn't know it, Bertrand had stopped the car five miles or so out of Bournsea, driven into a cutting by a farmgate and casually proceeded to light a cigarette. Then he lay back with half closed eyes in his seat and started concentrating. One thought was dominant; how he hated Cass; her large figure and bony face, her fads and fancies, and smirky looks when she set off in her car all painted up like some raddled hag to make mock of him behind his back. No subtlety, no quality, any more. No finesse.

He wished he'd never married her.

He wished she was dead.

Dead, dead, dead.

The word reiterated through his mind until the whole twilit landscape quivered with it and his ears and head swam with its buzzing echo . . . 'Cass. Dead . . . dead . . . '

His hands tingled to have them about her neck. Oh the sensuous awful satisfaction of it; to squeeze and press until she was nothing except a limp sack of unresisting garbage no longer able to taunt and annoy him.

The blood pounded and thudded through his arteries; darkness obliterated the misty landscape. A swimming curdling darkness that eventually resolved into a macabre distorted picture of Cass seated in his chair with greenish claw-like hands enclosing her throat. Dead, dead, he thought, and then suddenly it was over. The air cleared and the windscreen brightened from the fitful light of a climbing moon. He wiped his forehead with the clean pocket handkerchief from his pocket, smoothed his hair, and when the rapid beating of his heart had eased, started the engine of the car and set off again for Colonel Whitworth's.

Meanwhile, in the flat, Cassandra was sitting very still in the hated chair; the china figurine smashed to pieces on the floor. If a shadow loomed momentarily above her, obscene, luminously green skeletal hands clawing the air, no one saw. No one heard either, the vibrant crackle of sound holding the quality of malignant laughter before both finally disintegrated into general greyness and silence.

When found hours later by Bertrand, Cassandra's body had slumped sideways. It was cold, very cold. Her eyes were wide and staring, the tip of her tongue caught between her teeth.

At first it seemed to her husband there was a faint bruising around the throat, but when the police arrived it had faded.

Death was later recorded as one of natural causes, from a coronary, a view even Bertrand gulled himself into accepting, although he knew deep down the truth was very different.

He felt no guilt, telling himself that Cassandra had asked for what she'd got. However, from the moment of his wife's demise, the chair lost all fascination for him and after the funeral he sent it with other items to a local saleroom.

It fetched a comparatively small sum, considering its age and remarkable state of preservation.

'But then . . . ' one very elderly woman whispered to another as the auctioneer's hammer fell, 'you wouldn't expect it to, would you? Not with its history . . . ' The voice trailed off significantly.

'What history?' the other voice enquired. 'What do you mean?'

'Oh my dear! It was a murderer's chair. Didn't you know? But I suppose not, being new in these parts. Isaac Croker his name was . . . the man who made it. Jealous of his wife or something . . . a long time ago now, eighteen-something-or-other. He strangled her, not long after carving the thing. A real craftsman though, wood-worker. It's in the newspaper records they keep somewhere. Hanged he was. So . . . well, you can't exactly wonder that no one keeps it for long, can you? I mean a thing like that, with such hate worked into it. I can tell you I wouldn't take it as a gift. And it's funny two women have died in it. Or perhaps it isn't. That's not for me to say. The times I've watched that chair being bought and then come up again after a few months or a year or two, you wouldn't believe . . . '

There were other things too, that no one would have believed . . . in particular, the truth.

Other titles in the
Ulverscroft Large Print Series:

THE GREENWAY
Jane Adams

When Cassie and her twelve-year-old cousin Suzie had taken a short cut through an ancient Norfolk pathway, Suzie had simply vanished . . . Twenty years on, Cassie is still tormented by nightmares. She returns to Norfolk, determined to solve the mystery.

FORTY YEARS ON THE WILD FRONTIER
Carl Breihan & W. Montgomery

Noted Western historian Carl Breihan has culled from the handwritten diaries of John Montgomery, grandfather of co-author Wayne Montgomery, new facts about Wyatt Earp, Doc Holliday, Bat Masterson and other famous and infamous men and women who gained notoriety when the Western Frontier was opened up.

TAKE NOW, PAY LATER
Joanna Dessau

This fiction based on fact is the love-turning-to-hate story of Robert Carr, Earl of Somerset, and his wife, Frances.

McLEAN AT THE GOLDEN OWL
George Goodchild

Inspector McLean has resigned from Scotland Yard's CID and has opened an office in Wimpole Street. With the help of his able assistant, Tiny, he solves many crimes, including those of kidnapping, murder and poisoning.

KATE WEATHERBY
Anne Goring

Derbyshire, 1849: The Hunter family are the arrogant, powerful masters of Clough Grange. Their feuds are sparked by a generation of guilt, despair and ill-fortune. But their passions are awakened by the arrival of nineteen-year-old Kate Weatherby.

A VENETIAN RECKONING
Donna Leon

When the body of a prominent international lawyer is found in the carriage of an intercity train, Commissario Guido Brunetti begins to dig deeper into the secret lives of the once great and good.

A TASTE FOR DEATH
Peter O'Donnell

Modesty Blaise and Willie Garvin take on impossible odds in the shape of Simon Delicata, the man with a taste for death, and Swordmaster, Wenczel, in a terrifying duel. Finally, in the Sahara desert, the intrepid pair must summon every killing skill to survive.

SEVEN DAYS FROM MIDNIGHT
Rona Randall

In the Comet Theatre, London, seven people have good reason for wanting beautiful Maxine Culver out of the way. Each one has reason to fear her blackmail. But whose shadow is it that lurks in the wings, waiting to silence her once and for all?

QUEEN OF THE ELEPHANTS
Mark Shand

Mark Shand knows about the ways of elephants, but he is no match for the tiny Parbati Barua, the daughter of India's greatest expert on the Asian elephant, the late Prince of Gauripur, who taught her everything. Shand sought out Parbati to take part in a film about the plight of the wild herds today in north-east India.

THE DARKENING LEAF
Caroline Stickland

On storm-tossed Chesil Bank in 1847, the young lovers, Philobeth and Frederick, prevent wreckers mutilating the apparent corpse of a young woman. Discovering she is still alive, Frederick takes her to his grandmother's home. But the rescue is to have violent and far-reaching effects . . .

A WOMAN'S TOUCH
Emma Stirling

When Fenn went to stay on her uncle's farm in Africa, the lovely Helena Starr seemed to resent her — especially when Dr Jason Kemp agreed to Fenn helping in his bush hospital. Though it seemed Jason saw Fenn as little more than a child, her feelings for him were those of a woman.

A DEAD GIVEAWAY
Various Authors

This book offers the perfect opportunity to sample the skills of five of the finest writers of crime fiction — Clare Curzon, Gillian Linscott, Peter Lovesey, Dorothy Simpson and Margaret Yorke.

DOUBLE INDEMNITY
— MURDER FOR INSURANCE
Jad Adams

This is a collection of true cases of murderers who insured their victims then killed them — or attempted to. Each tense, compelling account tells a story of cold-blooded plotting and elaborate deception.

THE PEARLS OF COROMANDEL
By Keron Bhattacharya

John Sugden, an ambitious young Oxford graduate, joins the Indian Civil Service in the early 1920s and goes to uphold the British Raj. But he falls in love with a young Hindu girl and finds his loyalties tragically divided.

WHITE HARVEST
Louis Charbonneau

Kathy McNeely, a marine biologist, sets out for Alaska to carry out important research. But when she stumbles upon an illegal ivory poaching operation that is threatening the world's walrus population, she soon realises that she will have to survive more than the harsh elements . . .

TO THE GARDEN ALONE
Eve Ebbett

Widow Frances Morley's short, happy marriage was childless, and in a succession of borders she attempts to build a substitute relationship for the husband and family she does not have. Over all hovers the shadow of the man who terrorized her childhood.

CONTRASTS
Rowan Edwards

Julia had her life beautifully planned — she was building a thriving pottery business as well as sharing her home with her friend Pippa, and having fun owning a goat. But the goat's problems brought the new local vet, Sebastian Trent, into their lives.

MY OLD MAN AND THE SEA
David and Daniel Hays

Some fathers and sons go fishing together. David and Daniel Hays decided to sail a tiny boat seventeen thousand miles to the bottom of the world and back. Together, they weave a story of travel, adventure, and difficult, sometimes terrifying, sailing.

SQUEAKY CLEAN
James Pattinson

An important attribute of a prospective candidate for the United States presidency is not to have any dirt in your background which an eager muckraker can dig up. Senator William S. Gallicauder appeared to fit the bill perfectly. But then a skeleton came rattling out of an English cupboard.

NIGHT MOVES
Alan Scholefield

It was the first case that Macrae and Silver had worked on together. Malcolm Underdown had brutally stabbed to death Edward Craig and had attempted to murder Craig's fiancée, Jane Harrison. He swore he would be back for her. Now, four years later, he has simply walked from the mental hospital. Macrae and Silver must get to him — before he gets to Jane.

GREATEST CAT STORIES
Various Authors

Each story in this collection is chosen to show the cat at its best. James Herriot relates a tale about two of his cats. Stella Whitelaw has written a very funny story about a lion. Other stories provide examples of courageous, clever and lucky cats.

THE HAND OF DEATH
Margaret Yorke

The woman had been raped and murdered. As the police pursue their relentless inquiries, decent, gentle George Fortescue, the typical man-next-door, finds himself accused. While the real killer serenely selects his third victim — and then his fourth . . .

VOW OF FIDELITY
Veronica Black

Sister Joan of the Daughters of Compassion is shocked to discover that three of her former fellow art college students have recently died violently. When another death occurs, Sister Joan realizes that she must pit her wits against a cunning and ruthless killer.

MARY'S CHILD
Irene Carr

Penniless and desperate, Chrissie struggles to support herself as the Victorian years give way to the First World War. Her childhood friends, Ted and Frank, fall hopelessly in love with her. But there is only one man Chrissie loves, and fate and one man bent on revenge are determined to prevent the match . . .

THE SWIFTEST EAGLE
Alice Dwyer-Joyce

This book moves from Scotland to Malaya — before British Raj and now — and then to war-torn Vietnam and Cambodia . . . Virginia meets Gareth casually in the Western Isles, with no inkling of the sacrifice he must make for her.

VICTORIA & ALBERT
Richard Hough

Victoria and Albert had nine children and the family became the archetype of the nineteenth century. But the relationship between the Queen and her Prince Consort was passionate and turbulent; thunderous rows threatened to tear them apart, but always reconciliation and love broke through.

BREEZE: WAIF OF THE WILD
Marie Kelly

Bernard and Marie Kelly swapped their lives in London for a remote farmhouse in Cumbria. But they were to undergo an even more drastic upheaval when a two-day-old fragile roe deer fawn arrived on their doorstep. The knowledge of how to care for her was learned through sleepless nights and anxiety-filled days.

DEAR LAURA
Jean Stubbs
In Victorian London, Mr Theodore Crozier, of Crozier's Toys, succumbed to three grains of morphine. Wimbledon hoped it was suicide — but murder was whispered. Out of the neat cupboards of the Croziers' respectable home tumbled skeleton after skeleton.

MOTHER LOVE
Judith Henry Wall
Karen Billingsly begins to suspect that her son, Chad, has done something unthinkable — something beyond her wildest fears or imaginings. Gradually the terrible truth unfolds, and Karen must decide just how far she should go to protect her son from justice.

JOURNEY TO GUYANA
Margaret Bacon
In celebration of the anniversary of the emancipation of the African slaves in Guyana, the author published an account of her two-year stay there in the 1960s, revealing some fascinating insights into the multi-racial society.